MEN
FROM
CRIBAAR

MEN FROM CRIBAAR

LINDA SCHELL MOATS

iUniverse, Inc.
Bloomington

MEN FROM CRIBAAR

iUniverse books may be ordered through booksellers or by contacting:

iUniverse
1663 Liberty Drive
Bloomington, IN 47403
www.iuniverse.com
1-800-Authors (1-800-288-4677)

ISBN: 978-1-4502-6461-7 (sc)
ISBN: 978-1-4502-6462-4 (ebk)

Printed in the United States of America

iUniverse rev. date: 11/02/2011

I would like to acknowledge my friend, Ruthi Smith, for her assistance in getting my material in order.

PROLOGUE

I felt a hand on my back, a gentle but firm hand. I thought there was someone behind me, but everything happened so fast. I smelled what appeared to be burned rubber. I did not recognize the odor, and then I went blank. I could not remember being put on what I thought was an airplane, nor do I remember being put on a soft bed. I awoke briefly. I was laying face down. I tried to get up, but my arms were limp. I tried to move my legs but they would not respond. I called out to anyone that would listen to me, but I could not form my words. My voice came out like a pitiful cat sound. I could hear movements and then voices. I couldn't make out what they were saying but they were talking and laughing. Someone came back and touched my arm and asked if I was okay. He lifted me up and took me to the bathroom and sat me gently down. He left me alone for a few minutes and returned for me. He stroked my arm again. I could feel his touch. I struggled to get up and he told me to lie down and this would wear off in a day or two. *Who were these people?*

I found myself thinking. *What do they want with me?* I could only see his outline, everything was blurry. He told me to stay down that he didn't want me to get hurt. I could hear humming sounds. I tried to call out again, but only moaning sounds came out. *What is happening to me? Where am I?* Again, he stroked my arm and than my cheek. I tried to move away from him. I was not frightened, only upset with him. He told me that I would be okay and they would not harm me. He told me there were several other women on board. I thought about my husband and my children. They would be worried if I am gone too long. I thought about my friend Carrie, and what she would think if I did not show up. I have to get home now. I struggled again to get up, and the man picked up my hand and gently rubbed it until I fell back to sleep. I woke again, this time I could call out. The man came back to me again. He asked me if I wanted something to eat but I told him that I did not, and I only wanted him to take me home. He told me that we were almost there, and to sleep off the drug that they gave me and he would explain things later. He again told me they would not harm me. He stayed with me, and all I could think of, is what they were going to do to me. I was afraid they would rape and kill me. My body would be found in a ditch somewhere. Soon, I fell back to sleep.

CHAPTER ONE

"Where have you been?" John asked for the fifth time.

All I could do was stare at him. I had it all planned what I was going to say to him, but I could not get it out into words. Looking at him, I couldn't tell if he was mad, or was he just concerned?

"You've been gone for over two years and you don't have anything to say. You just appear out of nowhere and now you can't talk," he said vehemently. "What about your children. How can you do this to the children?"

"I'm not sure where I've been, John," I said as I looked deep into his eyes as if I was looking at a stranger instead of my husband for almost ten years. John is a very nice looking man, nicely built from working out at the gym. He is a lot shorter than his two brothers, and just slightly taller than I am. He looked the same as I remembered more than two years ago, except his hair is a bit more thin and graying. His eyes are big, and a beautiful blue, even though he had a frown now. I thought his eyes were his best feature. He was very easy going, to his friends and brothers but to me he was very commanding. He is a good father to our children. He was very stern with them but I know he loves them. He was always good to me and gave me anything I wanted, but we seemed to be at each others throats the last couple of years that we were together. We just didn't have as much in common as we use to. I felt us growing apart. He liked to go to the gym and spend a lot of time with his friends, but he mostly dwelled in his work. He had been drinking a lot more than when we were first married. I tried to talk to him about it so we could resolve the problems, but he didn't think we had problems. He just reminded me he has always loved me, and that should be enough. I just couldn't get the part where you could love someone so much that you spend more time away from them than you do together. I could not feel the closeness that we once had and I have been confused about my feelings for him. It was getting harder and harder to talk to him. When he was home he would spend a lot of time in his garage and work on his classic cars to avoid getting in a conversation with me. He usually told me that I was the only one that wasn't happy in this marriage. The more he drank and spent time away from home, the less I would talk to him about it. It would always turn into an argument like it was my fault. I guess I thought I could handle the situation as long as he was good to the children.

"Do you know that I have been searching for you? The police have been looking for your body Angie," he said in a much softer voice. "The children think that you left because you are mad at them and you didn't want them anymore. They have been so confused. Angie, please tell me where you were."

"I don't know John," I said again, "I was taken, I don't know where it was. John I was not taken by choice, I was captured." I had tears in my eyes and my body was shaking all over.

"Do you mean you were kidnapped?" He reached out to me, put his hand on my arm, but I took a step back. I just could not go into his arms. I had to get my feelings together knowing what I knew about him. It's been too long and I don't know if I can forgive him for what he had done, or for that matter, if he could forgive me. We have a lot to talk about before we can get back to normal.

"Talk to me Angie. What's going on? You're acting like we're strangers. You're my wife and I want to know where you have been all this time. I need to call the police to let them know you are back. Damn it Angie where have you been? I have missed you so much."

"Yes, I know, please don't call the police yet. John, I know we have to talk. Give us a chance to spend time together before calling the police. Where are the children? I want to see them."

"They have been staying with your parents. I couldn't take care of them and provide for them too. I've been spending a lot of time in the evenings searching for you. I followed up on every clue that I could find. Look Angie, if you were hurt, or if you were kidnapped, we need to get Sergeant Wayne here right now so we can get these guys before they do this to someone else." John said this almost like he doubted what I was telling him. He stared at me, frowning, even deeper than before. I knew he was frustrated. Maybe he does still care about me. I stood frozen for a few minutes thinking about the children staying with my parents. Andrew, almost nine and Alyssa, will be seven next month. I felt sick remembering my father being abusive toward me. He had no patience with me or my two brothers. I could not stand the idea of Andrew and Alyssa being with them and thinking that I was dead, or have abandon them. I told John that I was worried and he had a concerned look on his face. He was still frowning, as he answered.

"I go up every week-end and call them at least twice a week. I gave them a cell phone. They know they can call me at any time," John assured me. He was still watching me like if he stared at me long enough the truth would come out. "Your parents have been very good to them," he added.

"I want to go up now John, I have to see the children. That's all I could think about while I was gone John, please let's go now. I don't want them to be around my parents any more than they have to."

"Angie, I've got to be at work tomorrow. Let me tell them first. Come on, be realistic, I will call them tonight and let them and your parents know that you're home. If we go now, they will be even more confused. If you want to, you can talk to them on the phone to reassure them that you are okay. Angie your parents think you are dead and I don't doubt that is what she told the kids. I want to know every detail on how you got kidnapped and how you got away, and I want to know what they did to you. You owe me an explanation Angie."

I suddenly knew why John and I were having problems. I'd forgotten about how bad his controlling ways were. Everything had to go his way. Sometimes I felt like I was one of the children. During these last couple of years that I have been captured, I was treated like I was special even though at first it was not by choice. I was thinking about that when John took a hold of my arm again, and led me into the living room. John was a lot like my mother. You would have thought he was her son. I am very quiet and shy, and I lack self respect. I guess I allowed myself to be controlled by my parents and my husband. Whatever John asked me to do, or what to cook, I just did it to save from arguing with him. Whenever I didn't do something like he wanted it done, he would let me know in a very stern manner. I usually did not talk back to him just to keep peace.

I sat down and before taking a seat across from me, John turned around as if looking around the room to see if everything was in order. I looked around also. I couldn't help thinking how much bigger the house looked than I remembered. Everything was in neat order and very clean. I wondered if he had a housekeeper because he didn't do housework as long as I was around to do it. Everything was in it's place as much as I remembered. Pictures of the children lay on an end table next to some candle holders that I didn't remember having. I got up and walked over to pick up the two school pictures. I was shocked to see how much older and different the children looked. I missed them terribly and I told John that again as I held the pictures next to me.

"I would not have left the children, John. You and I have been having some problems and you know that. I have not been happy for a long time, but if I had left you by choice I would have taken the children with me."

"Come on, sit down," he said as he patted the seat next to him. "The kids are probably doing their chores right now. We have time to talk for a couple of hours before we call them. We will go out to get something to eat later, after I hear what you have to say," John said, again I thought a little controlling. "I just want to know where I stand right now, but tonight, we will have to call Sgt. Wayne to come over. You can tell him what happened. It's necessary Angie," John was talking as he got up and picked up my hand, took the pictures from me, and put them on the same table where I got them from, adjusting them as he did. He then led me to the sofa like I had to tell him everything before I was allowed to look at the pictures, or go out to eat.

"I tried to find you Angie. The police call me often when they find clues. They keep me informed of what is going on. There were over three hundred women missing the same month that you disappeared. All of them were from different states. Did you know that?"

Before I had a chance to answer, he went on. "There were several meetings with the police and other family members of women that were missing. We were trying to figure out if there were similar things that happened. It seems that all of them were married and had one to three children. They disappeared within three days of each other. At first, I thought you were upset with me for some reason. I had a hard time making myself believe that you would leave the children. Then we thought you were kidnapped and taken to some cult, or used as a slave or something like that. After a year of searching we started to think something else happened. The police looked for bodies, but only a few were found. Neither one of those women had children, so there was no connection. We were all baffled and couldn't come up with any clues. I told the police that you would not have left the children on your own free will. Other families said the same thing. I was even a suspect in your disappearance, but I was cleared because of no body and no evidence. I took a lie detector test and I'm sure that the others went through the same thing. God, Angie, I went through hell. I didn't think I was ever going to see you again."

I don't remember John talking this much to me since we were teenagers. "I'm sorry John. I didn't mean to worry you. I missed you and the kids. I was not in a cult, but I was in a strange place. John, please, I don't want to talk about it anymore now. I promise I will tell you, but right now I just want to take a long hot bath. I'm very tired and I just want to get use to being back. I need to get my thoughts together. I want to sleep and I don't want anything to eat," I said in a pleading manner. All I could think was, no wonder they thought he was guilty. They probably found out that there were other women in his life.

"Okay Honey," John said, although I could see that he was not pleased. "Can I at least call Sergeant Wayne and let him know that you are back? You go ahead and take your bath. Let me know when you are finished and we will call the children."

"Okay," I agreed.

I got up and slowly walked toward the stairs. I turned around, and he was looking at me. I could see the concerned look in his face, although partly anguished. He was studying me.

"I'm sorry!" I said again.

"Angie are the other women back?"

"Most of them, some chose to stay."

"What do you mean some chose to stay? Does that mean you and the other women actually enjoyed being where you were?"

"We were treated with love and respect John." I walked back again to pick up the children's pictures. I looked at them again, and decided to take them upstairs with me. John didn't take them back from me this time.

"They allowed us to come back because of the children. I had to see if we can make our marriage work. I have a lot of questions for you too."

"What took you so long? Why after all this time did you want to see if you still care enough for me to see if we can make our marriage work?" He said this with disgust. I was getting mixed emotions from him.

"We couldn't leave if we wanted to. I will explain all that to you later when we talk to the police."

"Do you want me to do anything for you? I could bring you a nice cup of hot tea or something."

"Yes, thanks," I said, almost in a whisper. "That would be nice." I thought of saying something more and I think he realized it, but I decided not to get into another confrontation with him. He never wanted to bring me anything before. I lingered a couple of seconds more, and then slowly turned around and climbed the stairs. I could feel his eyes follow me. I didn't know what else to say or have the energy to go on just now.

If I took my things into the guest room, John would be mad or maybe even cause an argument. He would suspect something was wrong between us. I decided to stay in our room, although; that is not what I wanted to do. I walked over to the dresser next to my side of the bed and set the pictures down. My things were still there just as I left them. I opened all my drawers and looked to see if I remembered everything. It didn't look like anything had been touched. Strange, I would have thought my drawers would have been gone through, looking for clues of my whereabouts. I took my brush in my hand and studied myself in the mirror. As I was running the brush through my long, thick, dark hair, I was checking the way I looked. I didn't feel like I was attractive, cute maybe, but I was far from beautiful. My eyes were green and wide. I always wished they were brown or blue. I had nice full lips but I thought my face was far too thin. Although I had good skin, it was no match for Carrie's. My wonderful friend Carrie, so beautiful, I miss her. First thing tomorrow, I will call her.

I had just finished my shower and wrapped my wet hair in a towel, with barely enough time to slip my robe on when John brought the tea up. He placed it on the dresser by the bed. He turned toward me and looked at me up and down. I could see desire in his eyes as I quickly pulled my robe shut. I was not ready for him and I think he felt that.

"I called Sergeant Wayne. He wanted to come out immediately but I told him you were tired. I think he understands that you would be able to help them more in the morning. I will go in the office late so I can be here when he comes. He'll be here around ten. Angie are we okay? I love you, you know that don't you? I never once stopped loving you." He took a couple of steps toward me. I was afraid that he was going to put his arms around me. I again stepped back from him. I was overcome by a sudden chill. *Yea right*, I thought, *you love me so much that you cheated on me.*

"Of course we're okay John. At least I think so. Maybe you will feel differently after you hear what I have to tell you." I could only think, *no John, we are not alright. We probably never were. Maybe, never will be.* "I will sleep in the guest room if you want me to."

"Why would you even think that? We're still married even if you were gone half of our married life. Tell me now if there is someone else, Angie." Again I detected a little anger in his voice.

"John you're acting like I did something wrong. I didn't have a choice and I need you to believe me." I said this with a little frustration in my voice and he backed off. I slowly sipped the tea and sat down on the bed. He didn't answer me so I had no idea what he was thinking. I wanted to wait for the right time to tell him the truth and what I knew about him. He threw his hands deeply in his pocket jingling his change. This was a nervous habit he had when he was frustrated. He then removed his cell phone from his belt and started dialing.

"I'll get the children on the phone," he said, not even looking my way.

I wondered how much the children had changed and if they would accept me back into their lives. I thought about them everyday while I was gone, wondering what they look like and what they were doing. I would picture their faces as they became older. How I hated missing this part of their growing up.

"Hi Alyssa," John said, sounding cheerful. "I love you too sweetie. Honey is your brother nearby? I need to talk to him about something. I know Honey, but I will talk to you next. This is very important. Andrew, how are you doing? Listen to me guy, I need you to listen to what I have to say. Your mother has been found. Yes, she is okay. Yes, she is right here. No, I will bring her up this week-end and you can spend time with her. Do you want to talk to her?"

I could feel my heart pounding as I said hello to him. "Are you doing okay son?"

"Hi Mom, I'm doing fine. Where were you Mom?" I could tell that he was crying.

"Andrew, I will tell you about it when I get there this week-end."

"Mom, I want to come home now," he said in a voice that I did not recognize. He has changed and I missed it. He sounded so much more grown up. They were both very smart and did wonderful in school. They were a joy to us and I have been so lucky to have two special children. Jonathon Andrew Marcus was named after his father and looked just like him. He had beautiful blue eyes and a nice smile. He has always been a sweet child and Alyssa Lyn, took more after me, even my green eyes and thin face. She was tiny framed where Andrew was built like his father. They both were always very helpful and sweet. Alyssa seemed never to have a care in the world. This past year, I would think of her giggling over the most simple things and it always brought a smile to my face. Thinking of my children is what kept me going these past two and a half years.

"Mommy and Daddy have to talk to the police and tell them what happened so they may be able to help others. But I promise you we will be there this week-end to see you. I love you and I've missed you so much. I want you and Alyssa back with me as soon as possible. We will talk about your coming home when we get there. I need you to talk to Alyssa, and tell her what I told you. Do you understand Andrew?"

"Okay Mom!" he said. I could tell he was not happy.

"You sound so grown up honey. I can't wait to see you. I have your pictures here with me, holding them, so I can look at them until I get there. I'm sending you a big hug through the phone. Are you ready to catch it?"

"Thanks Mom, I got it."

"Okay honey, I love you. Put your grandmother on the phone. Your dad wants to talk to her."

John took the phone from me and walked out of the room. All I could hear him say was "Yes Myra, she is really back, I don't know, I don't know," as he walked slowly down the stairs. I felt that he had a lot more to say to her after he left me alone.

John came up to bed later and I pretended to be asleep. I just did not want to talk to him right now. He slipped his arm around me, and I felt his breath on my neck. He snuggled very close to me. I became frightened that he would want me to make love with him. I could tell that he had been drinking, and that usually meant that he would push his advances on me even if I was not ready. A few months before my disappearance, the only time we made love was when he was drinking and that was to satisfy himself only. I couldn't help to think that I hope he could not feel me shiver. I guess he decided not to push himself on me yet, because he soon fell asleep. Although I was very tired, I could not sleep. I thought about things that happened the last two and a half years and how I was going to explain it.

CHAPTER TWO

"Come in Grant," I heard John saying. I was not ready for this, but I knew I had to get it over with. I knew that no one was going to believe me. It helped knowing that three hundred other women went through the same thing as I did. Maybe it will help make what really happened more believable.

"Can I get you a cup of coffee?" I asked him after I entered the front room and gave him a hug.

"That would be nice," Grant looked back at me as he took a seat. "Angie, I'm so glad that you are okay. We've all been so worried. You look great, but you have lost a lot of weight."

"I'll get us some coffee." John quickly walked to the kitchen, as if he would miss something if he was gone too long.

I sat down next to Grant Wayne, still thinking, I don't know where to start.

"You look great," he said again.

We've known Grant since we were kids. John, Grant, Carrie and I all went to school together. We all took up for each other through rough times. We would all go to the Dellie, a small diner where all the local teens would hang out listen to music and drink cherry cokes. We would tell each other our secrets and laugh together.

"Thanks Grant, you look the same too." Although I have known him for years, I felt very nervous.

"Angie I want to make this as easy for you as possible."

I almost believed that he felt sorry for me. Grant was always the help people type. We always went to him with our problems, and he always seemed to have the answers. He had a crush on me as we were growing up, but would not dare ask me out. Nobody ever took anything or anyone away from John. John and I loved each other since we were kids, so I thought.

"Are all the other women that are missing back too?" he asked.

"Most of them."

"I want you to think back to the morning you disappeared. You got the kids off to school. You had some shopping to do. The last you were seen is when you walked out of the grocery store. You were suppose to go to Carrie's but you never showed up. At first Carrie thought you got stuck in traffic or something, but after about an hour and a half she became frantic and called John, and he got in touch with us. She tried to call you several times and even came back here thinking you got hurt, and maybe couldn't get to the phone."

"I'm sorry, I remember walking over to my car," I was trying to remember some of the unimportant details. "I remember seeing some kind of flash and it frightened me. I didn't know what it was. I guess he used something to make me pass out because I couldn't remember much right after the flash."

"What did the flash look like?" John interrupted as he entered the room carrying a tray of coffee and muffins.

"I don't know! I never saw anything like it before. Just a bright yellow flash like someone with a very large camera. I didn't have time to think. I remember smelling something like rubber burning. I think I woke up several hours later. It sounded like a humming noise and I could hear some people talking but I couldn't make out what they were saying."

John sat down in a chair across from me. "Were you in a car or what?"

"No John, It was something much bigger. I honestly thought at the time that I was in an airplane, but I found out later that it was something from another world." There, I said it, but I knew instantly they did not believe me. I looked at John and then back at Grant.

They looked at each other in disbelief, and then they both looked at me. Grant, with his winning smile and John just stared at me.

"You did want the truth didn't you Grant?" I went on as he nodded his head. "We took hours to get to where we were going or maybe another day. I think we were moving fast. Listen, I know this all sounds ridiculous but this is what happened. I couldn't believe it myself at first."

"Angie" Grant leaned back in his chair with his hands behind his head. "Are you trying to tell us that you were in some kind of UFO?" He said this smiling at John.

"That's what I'm trying to tell you Grant. How else could you explain three hundred women missing? Do you think I could have planned all that? I can't go on if you're going to take this as a joke."

"Go on," John was grinning and I knew he was not taking me seriously. "I want to hear this." He put his hands up toward Grant. I thought John looked handsome this morning. He was much better looking than Grant but Grant had a loving personality. I would say he was very cute. He had put on a few pounds since I saw him last but it only improved his good looks. He had a very warm smile using it now to show his confusion. His brown, natural wavy hair is longer, otherwise, he looked about the same as I remembered. Right now he had a concerned look on his face.

"The men look the same as they do here. They talk with some kind of strange accent. Their place looks a bit like ours only more colorful. Their buildings are dome in shape. Their homes inside are circular but not as large as our homes. They have more glass in theirs. There is no kitchen because no one cooks at home." I found myself avoiding telling them everything right now. I just wanted this to be over. The secrets would have to come out later. I wanted right now to talk to Carrie. She's the only one that I could confide in. We told each other everything. She's the only one, besides my mother and Grant, that knows that John and I are having problems. Carrie and I are never critical of each other. We just listen and offer some advice. I knew that she never cared much for John. She said that he is too much of a flirt, even flirting with her. She told me numerous times she didn't like the way he treated me, and he didn't have much respect for me.

"Do you know why they held you for almost two and a half years?" Grant asked when there was a long pause after my description of the strangers houses. "Did they do some kind of experiment or hurt you in any way?"

I dreaded this part so I decided to evade the question until I could talk to Carrie and John.

"It's a long story," I said. "I think it was more like what they wanted from us, but they did not hurt us. They are very gentle men. They treated us with respect. Right now you have the most important parts. I think most of the women will be cooperative and we can fill you in with more detail later. I think you will find that all our stories are similar."

We talked about fifteen minutes longer before Grant got a call and had to get back to his office.

"Okay, Angie," Grant got up to leave. "I will have more questions later. I will get in touch with some other families of missing wives and maybe we can have a meeting. Maybe you should keep this to yourself for now. This kind of thing could start a panic if it gets out. You don't want that."

"Call later when you find out anything," John said as he followed Grant to the door. "I will be at the office at least until six."

"Angie one more thing, you said that most of the women are back. Where are the rest of them?" Grant asked as he opened the door to leave.

"Some were having problems with their husbands and were close to a divorce, so they chose to stay where they took us."

"Did you actually talk to the others?"

"Yes, I got to know some and most of us ate at the same time at a large dining room."

I felt that John wanted to talk to Grant while I was not around, but that's okay. I wanted him to leave so that I could talk to Carrie.

"Are you okay, Angie? I have to leave for work, but if you don't want to be alone, I can call Carrie or someone," John said as he quickly checked himself in the hall mirror.

"No, no," I said quickly, "I'll be fine. I will call Carrie to let her know that I'm back."

"Okay, I'll call you later." John grabbed up his things and quickly slipped out the door without saying goodbye. I knew he wanted to catch up with Grant.

As soon as he was out of sight I called Carrie.

"Hi Carrie, this is Angie"

"Angie, where are you? Where have you been? We've been so worried, are you okay?" Carrie is so sweet and thoughtful. I thought she was going to end up with Grant Wayne. They dated for a while but she went off to college and met Brian and later they got married. Grant never married, he said his job is too dangerous and he stays very busy. Brian is crazy about Carrie. I always thought they had the most perfect marriage of any couple I ever knew. He showered her with love and attention, and was always bringing her gifts. They have been married for almost six years now. Brian and Carrie doted on my children because they could not have children of their own. I loved being around them. They always seemed to be excited about things and always joking with each other. Brian is tall and thin, not really good looking, but his personality made up for that. I always thought Carrie was knock out gorgeous with her very dark hair and large brown eyes. I felt I was very plain looking next to Carrie.

"I'm okay Carrie, but I need to talk to you. I don't have a car anymore. Can you come over now? I will explain everything to you."

"Of course I will come over. I can't wait to see you. I'll be there in about twenty minutes." Carrie rang the doorbell in less than fifteen minutes. She grabbed me up and held me tightly.

"I didn't think I was ever going to see you again." She cried, and then we both stood there and cried.

She looked the same as always, beautiful and much younger looking than she really was. Her long hair was pulled back in a pony tail. Her beautiful wide eyes misty with tears. I told her she looked like she lost some weight and she told me that it was because she thought she had lost her best friend. She cried again while I was crying with her.

"I called Brian," she said. "He knows that you are okay. Angie where were you? I missed you terribly."

"Gosh, I got more of a welcome from you than I did John. Come on in, I'll fix us some coffee, and boy do I have some things to tell you. Come on, let's go in the kitchen like old times." I repeated what I told the men this morning. "But there is more Carrie. I didn't tell them everything. I wanted to talk to you first. I just don't know if I should tell John everything. He may not understand. He is acting strange like he doesn't believe me. Carrie do you believe me?"

"Well it is a little strange but Angie, I've got to say maybe you were drugged and confused of what really happened. Maybe they brain washed you or something, but I know that you have never lied to me."

"No Carrie, I was drugged at first, but so help me what I am telling you is the truth. You see at first I thought that the men were kidnapping women and using them for their own purpose to make money. That was not the case at all. But, I need to start from the beginning."

"Miim is his name. He is the one who took me but other men took the other women. They live on a tiny planet they call Cribaar. When I woke up from a deep sleep, he asked me if I was okay. He gave me something to eat. It was yellow and very good but I didn't recognize it. I asked him where I was and when he told me I didn't believe him. He looked just like any other man that I know, except extremely handsome, tall, nice build. He didn't look like the kind of guy that would go around kidnapping women, and I told him that. I asked him again where I was and when he told me I still didn't believe him. I said to him, "look unless you have a very good reason to keep me here, you better put me back where I was. I am married and have two children, and they will miss me."

"They already miss you," he said in a very strong accent. "You have been gone almost three days."

"What do you want with me?" This time I was mad as fear swept over me. I told him several times to put me back that I didn't believe him, and I didn't want to be there. He said he would talk to me later and tell me all about it, for now he just wanted me to rest. If I didn't know better, I thought he was very kind and almost sweet. He seemed to be very concerned about me. Deep lines fell into his forehead as he was talking. He appeared to be the type of man that most women fall for. He had the most beautiful smile I had ever seen. Dimples present when he smiled and he had nice straight teeth. His hair was dark, curly, not long, but long enough to mold slightly over his neck.

I felt like he had to tell me some things that were very important. He walked over to a large circular window, pushed a button, and daylight came through.

"Look," he said, "I want to show you that I am telling you the truth."

I stood up, still feeling dizzy and uncoordinated. I walked slowly to the window a bit wobbly. He stretched out his arms to me to keep me from falling, and I took his hand as he gently walked me to the window. The things I saw were so unreal. All the buildings were round and everything was white, even the hills behind the buildings were white. I saw rails above buildings that looked like monorails in a theme park. I could see strange looking cars moving on them and I could not grasp the things I saw. I felt my knees buckle under me and Miim grabbed me up in his arms and gently laid me down on the large circular bed.

"This looks like something out of a movie. I keep thinking I'm in a bad dream."

"I'm sorry," he said with a lot of sincerity. "I don't want to harm you in any way. Just lie down and when you are completely recovered, I will explain everything to you. Please don't be afraid of me or our planet. I don't want you hurt and I want you to believe me when I say we care about you."

"You are telling me the truth," I said to him still feeling very confused. "This is another planet and you are an alien."

"Yes it is the truth," he said as he stroked my hair and I tried moving further back from him. I did not want him to touch me. "I'm not sure if I am the alien though."

"Honestly Carrie, I was so tired and confused. I was not at all frightened of this man. He was so kind and concerned about me and actually joking with me. We talked about his planet for about fifteen minutes. He explained to me how they built their town in the mountain, and the rails were for their cars. Their mountains were like white marble. Their bathrooms were made from the material they called rovant, material that came from the mountains. They also used it in their walkways. They had no soil as we know it. They grew everything in hothouses and used a white, powdery substance that resembled soil to grow some of their fruits and vegetables. I found what he was saying very interesting, but as he was talking I drifted off to sleep.

The next morning he came in again. He gave me some fresh clothes, and told me where I could clean up. He showed me where the bathroom was, and how to work the bath then he left. I looked around the bath area. It was pretty and it looked like marble. It was very large and you had to walk down the stairs to get into the water. It was warm and soft and so peaceful. I didn't want to get out, it just felt so good. There were several buttons and I wondered what they were for. I dried off with a warm soft cloth and dressed in some kind of wrap. It also felt very soft and warm. I felt at peace. I found myself looking around the room. There were tall glass containers with something in them and they were all different colors and very pretty. There was a large room with a curtain on it which I found out later was for heat and massages for sore muscles.

Later, Miim came back into the bedroom to get me, knocking as he did so, and took me out into a different room. Everything in that room was golden in color. I guessed it to be a sitting area, but everything was round. The lighting was soft and it was so beautiful and had a serenity about it. When he asked me to sit, I chose a small round chair that looked more like our bucket seat. I again felt comfort like I have never felt before. He was pacing up and down the room like he was wondering where to begin. He looked very serious, almost hurt. He offered me food from a tray but I refused and told him I just wanted coffee. He said they didn't have anything like that, but he gave me a glass of what I guessed to be juice.

"You must eat, you will feel much better and you will be able to think more clearly, yes?" I noticed then that he used "yes," after sentences he wanted me to answer yes and "no," to sentences he wanted me to say no. He looked at me, and again I felt peace like I knew he was not going to hurt me. I again, could tell he was very concerned about me. I asked him what he wanted with me. This time with a bit more anger. He said that he was sorry to have frightened me and that was not what they intended. He also told me if there was any other way they could have handled the situation, they would have done it. He asked me if I needed anything and wanted to make sure I was comfortable. He then asked me if I was feeling better and I asked him to please go on because I needed to know why I was here, and what they wanted from me. Carrie, he told me a story that is so unbelievable. I sometimes wonder about if myself, but it is true. This is what he told me."

CHAPTER THREE

"I have been studying you for several months now," Miim said, as he got comfortable in a chair next to me. "I know that you are married to John and have two children, Andrew and Alyssa. They are in grade school. I know that you go grocery shopping every Tuesday and you go out every Thursday for other chores. You have a friend named Carrie and you meet her for lunch after your chores on Thursdays. She comes over at your house at least once a week and stays about an hour. Your Doctor is Dr. Vaughn. He delivered your children. I also know that you want more children and John does not. Your marriage has not been the greatest, but I know that you love your children dearly, yes?"

"How dare you to stalk me like that. How do you know all of this?" I asked sternly. "You know as much about me as my friend does."

"I have been to your planet for the last two years trying to find just the right person to bring back with me. I have been studying you, and you were the perfect person."

"But I'm married and I have children. How can I be the right person to bring back? What do you want with me? You have no right to take me away if I don't want to go."

"That's what made you right Angie," he said, in an ever so sweet voice, "Because you do have children and you are married. I have been searching for you for several months when I found you at your Doctor's office. I found out there that you are still able to have children. I know this will be hard on your children, but your husband does not have the respect he should have for you, no? He hollers at you like you are one of the children. He orders you around and pushes you like you are one of his slaves instead of his wife. He just might have more love and respect for you after you are gone awhile. I promise I will return you if you want, but I can't right now."

"Wait a minute. Do you mean to tell me that your planet kidnaps people and holds them until you decide that their family is suffering enough, and then you return them? Don't you guys know that's against the law? And what right do you have spying on my personal life? How do you know what my husband is like?"

"After you hear what I have to tell you, maybe you will understand that we don't have a choice and no we are not trying to punish anyone. I selected you because you can have children and want more. I hear when your husband takes you out to dinner and talks to you badly. Your marriage is not good. You are very good to him and kind, not to mention, you are very beautiful and well shaped, yes."

"Are you trying to tell me that you guys stole me so I can have a baby up here? Well you can guess again. Do you know that is called rape and you could be punished for this? You told me yourself that no harm would come to me."

"And I meant it. I promise I will not try to harm you. Again, I am trying to tell you we have no choice so we will not be punished for kidnapping, and I do not plan to rape you. I am hoping you will understand after I tell you our story and you will cooperate with me, and then I will return you."

"It still sounds like a threat to me like you are not going to let me go until I have your baby or something. This is all too eerie."

"Please listen to me. It's not exactly like that. I want to wait until you're ready. I do not want to take you against your will, but you have to know this is necessary. This is the only thing that will save our planet."

I could not believe what he was saying. How could I save his planet? Things were starting to get pretty creepy. This dude actually thought that I could have his baby, and that was not wrong? At this point I was getting mad, I did not fear him, I was just mad.

"And what if I refuse? What if I am never ready? Does that mean that I can never go home?" This time he knew that I was not very happy.

"I am hoping you will understand after I tell you the reason you are here. You see, about five years ago we lost all of our women and female children to a terrible illness. The male children and men survived. At first we did not understand it, but after research we found a cure. By then it was too late. All of our females were gone. This can happen on your planet as well as it did on our planet. If it did, it would end all mankind unless there was another way to produce women again. We need females as well as males, but more importantly, at this point, we need females. The youngest boys on our planet right now are almost six years old and our time is running out. We took over three hundred women from Earth to help us to start a new generation."

"Where are the other women you took from Earth?" I asked, almost concerned about what he was telling me but still unable to grasp it. "I didn't know there was another planet."

"The other women are with different men. I will take you to where we meet to eat our meals and you will get a chance to talk to them and meet some other men on our planet."

"Where did you guys come from?"

"We are a tiny planet, I'm sure you didn't even know we existed, because we hid behind your much larger planets. We know more about you than you know about us. We are much like you because we believe that in a period of time, we came from Earth. That is why we need Earth women. More then five hundred years ago, our ancestors came here to start a perfect world, after much corruption on Earth. I know that all of this does not make sense to you right now, but you will understand as time goes by. I know that you have a lot of questions, but we will answer them tonight after our meal."

"Well tell me this, do you plan for all these women to get pregnant artificially or do you plan to have sex with us?"

"Boy you Earth women sure put things bluntly don't you? In answer to your question, we have no choice but to come together as man and wife. I can get you a legal divorce and we can be married if that is what you want. Our laws are different from your laws, so that would not be a problem."

"You are not getting this. I just want you to take me home right now. I do not want a divorce nor do I want to marry you. As I matter of fact, I refuse to have a baby with you, so you might as well go ahead and take me back home."

"I am sorry but you will have to stay away at least two years, so you just might at least think about it. You will be able to leave with the rest of the women."

"And what if I run away, what would you do?"

"Where will you go, Angie? There is only one way off of this planet. I have a feeling you would not be able to figure that out on your own. The men on this planet are not going to help you. We are desperate and need your help. There is no choice here for you. I'm just asking for your understanding and cooperation."

"Well you sure as hell will not get that. You guys have just assumed that you can have your way with us, and expected us to say it's alright. I thought you said this is a perfect world. Well listen to me, committing rape is not perfect."

"Angie, you don't understand. It has nothing to do with having our way. Doesn't anything I said make sense to you? Don't you understand that if we didn't do this we are a lost planet?"

"Well what about the artificial way. Why do we need to commit adultery, or better yet why don't all you guys just come on back to Earth and meet nice single women?"

"In the first place, many years ago we had the choice to use artificial means but we decided against it because it was against our beliefs. Now it is too late to begin again. Another reason is because we need to be reasonably sure that we can have children right away. Artificial insemination can take a long time and because our forefathers thought it was wrong, we don't know much about it. Time is something we don't have. As far as our men going to earth to live, that's out of the question. Meeting single women would only delay our efforts, especially when we don't even know if they can have children. We need a perfect world to live in and earth people are corrupt. Do you really believe they would accept us?"

"What am I suppose to tell my husband when I get back? He will ask where I have been all this time. Am I suppose to tell him I was on some other planet, having some other man's baby? Do you really expect him to believe me? Do you think he would take me back?"

"It does not matter what you tell him, the truth if you want to. Earth will know about us sooner or later. Your husband is not exactly the most innocent person on Earth."

"What do you mean?"

"I mean, he has cheated on you more than once. That is another reason why I chose you. He does not care for you."

"Yea, right, do you expect me to believe you? This is your way of saying if he cheated on me then it's okay if I cheat on him."

"Well no, although it does sound like a good way to get you to cooperate. You deserve to be treated with more love and respect than he gives you. You understand this, yes? I am telling you the truth. We are not in a habit of lying up here, and we are faithful to our women."

"Do you know who he cheated on me with?" Still not believing him, but at the same time thinking this could be a possibility. I could feel the tears welling up in my eyes.

"Yes, do you want to know?"

"Well you told me he cheated on me, you may as well tell me the rest."

"Don't you think that he and Kay have been spending a lot of time together?"

"That doesn't mean they sleep together. They do work together and maybe go out to lunch. It's business."

"Maybe these will prove they have been having more than lunch together."

Miim showed me pictures of intimate hugs, and there, John was kissing Kay. Not just a sweet parting kiss. This was a kiss of wanting and passion. There was also pictures of them going into a motel. They had on different clothes in each picture, proof that this was not a one time affair. I was shocked. I just stared at the pictures with disbelief and in total shock. How could this total stranger know about this and I wouldn't even have guessed?

"How could he do this to me?" I cried. "I trusted him, I trusted him with all my heart. How could he do this to me?" Kay is John's secretary, and although she is somewhat attractive, I never thought they would ever be lovers. Kay is tall and thin, even taller than John. She kept her hair on top of her head, it was blond and she did have nice blue eyes. I thought she was very business like, and always put her job first. She is not married right now.

John told me she has been married twice but divorced both times after short marriages. I could not imagine the two together. She seemed to be a bit of a snob, and I suspected that she didn't like me, but Kay would be the last person, I thought, would go after my husband or my husband would go after her. John even complained about her on occasion, but maybe that was because he didn't want me to think there was anything going on. I couldn't help but to wonder how long this has been going on.

Miim reached for me to console me, but I turned away from him I did not want him or any one else to touch me. Right now, I just didn't trust anyone. He must have sensed it because he said that he was sorry and he understood why I didn't trust him, or maybe these guys can read minds. I cried for about five minutes and not once did he move. He just sat with me like he understood me. I tried to think back to the times when John came home late from work. I always thought if he ever cheated on me, I would know. He would leave some kind of clue. He was very careless. I knew our marriage had some problems, but I truly thought that he loved me enough not to cheat on me. Now I know that he did not, and I question myself on how much I really loved him. I felt so stupid.

"Do you know how long he has been cheating on me?" I asked Miim.

"At least two years, since I have been on Earth. I don't know how much longer."

I sat there at least another twenty minutes crying and thinking about how I missed the signs. Miim was very patient sitting with me not saying anything else until I spoke again.

"Do you read minds too?" I started to giggle, crying at the same time.

"No, we do not read minds," he laughed with me. "We are just a fun loving and caring type of people. We are a lot like you but we do have more moral beliefs. We think this is a perfect world, no thieves, murderers and no one cheats or lies here. Until this strange illness that took our women happened, no harm came to us. We are mostly healthy and life expectancy here is much longer than Earth's. We have Doctors and accidents do happen. I'm not telling you that we don't have disagreements but we always manage to come to some conclusion that is going to satisfy most people. We love it here and if you give us a chance, I think you will too.

I wanted to reach out to him, only because I needed a friend right now, or maybe I did want more. I felt unsure about my feelings. I knew that I needed to get them straight before I did anything I would be sorry for. Again, he seemed to sense my feelings.

"I'm sorry, I am, I just think your men need to be more honest than they are. Women deserve to be treated with love, kindness and respect and not cheated on."

"Did you plan to use this information and pictures if you knew I would not cooperate with you?"

"No, I planned to tell you whether you cooperated or not. I wanted to give you more time to adjust before telling you. I knew you would be hurt, but all lies must be known and dealt with."

"I guess I just never thought about that before. This does sound like a perfect world to live in."

"Almost, listen, I laid some clothes out for you on your bed. Why don't you get dressed up and we will go get something to eat. It will give you a chance to talk to some other women and meet some more of us. Angie, I want to help you. If you need to talk, let me know. I will try to help you through this."

"Thanks," I said, as I slowly walked towards the room he put me in, without glancing back. I could feel his eyes following me and I knew he was genuinely concerned.

I found a dress neatly strewn across the bed. A pretty multicolor one with wavy lines. Not something I would have picked out for myself but it looked great. Near the bed I found some sandals that were gray in color but matched the dress nicely. I checked myself in a mirror, my face paler than usual, and my eyes puffy. I took my make-up from my purse and applied some lightly. I then ran a comb through my hair and applied some hand cream on my hands. When I finished I thought I looked pretty good except a little puffy around the eyes from crying. I went back out to the sitting area and waited for Miim. I looked around the room and found the things very interesting but almost masculine in decor. A neat looking rock, that looked almost like a volcano, sat on a shelf with some bottles that looked like they were made of ivory. There was very little furniture, maybe enough chairs to seat four people and a table that looked like it was made of ivory. I noticed the lighting was recessed in the dome ceiling. There were drapery that almost looked like real gold, on the whole length of the wall. It was so beautiful. I also noticed some pictures of some beautiful women that were sitting on a stand. I walked over to them, and I was intrigued by their beauty. They both had eyes and a smile very much like Miim's. I wondered if one of them was Miim's wife and I instantly felt sorry for him. I wondered what it was that took their lives at such an early life.

"Wow," Miim said as he walked in with a smile, "You look great! Pretty good fit for not knowing your size. Are you ready to go eat?"

"This is not a date is it?"

"No, not if you don't want it to be, but there is nothing here to eat, except snacks, so we have to go to the dining room." He reached out for my hand but I refused it. I walked over to where I thought the door was, but there was no doorknob. He pushed a button and another area in the room slid open. I was a little embarrassed.

"I guess I couldn't have escaped if I wanted to," I said teasingly. As he smiled down at me, I couldn't help noticing how good he looked. He probably would never have noticed me if I had met him home. His clothes were not unlike what our own men would wear, only he wore them more strikingly. Under normal circumstances I would have been very proud to be seen with him. Secretly, I thought the date thing sounded good, but I quickly shifted my thoughts just in case these people could read minds. He put his hand gently under my arm and guided me to another area with a sliding door.

As we stepped outside for the first time since I have been here, I noticed again that all the houses had a round shape, white and some cream in color. Everything was neat, tidy, no trash or dirt anywhere. There were no trees or shrubbery that I could see and I asked Miim about it. He told me there was a park that had a lot of greenery. He told me he would like to show it to me someday. He led me to a vehicle that was a grayish white and almost circular. When he got me in the vehicle and came around to the other side, he stepped in and pushed a button. I guess we were on a rail because it drove itself. There was no steering wheel, just buttons.

"You may as well relax," he said with a grin, "this takes about five minutes."

"How does this work? I asked.

"Uh huh, now you want to go back to Earth with all our secrets."

"No, I probably would not understand anyway."

"Just kidding, it's something like your electricity but a bit more complicated. One day I will explain it to you on paper. You look beautiful in that dress that I picked out for you."

"Thank you! How did you know my size?"

"Good guess, or maybe I inquired in the stores that you and Carrie shop in."

"Which one?"

"Which one what?"

"Did you guess or did you ask at the store?"

He just looked down at me and smiled. I guess he felt better than to answer. I returned his smile.

"Miim, I saw a picture of two beautiful women in your house. Was one of them your wife?"

"No, that was my mother and sister. I lost them to the illness."

"I'm sorry, were you ever married?"

"No, I have never found that right person. Of course I thought I had plenty of time to fall in love."

"Your mother looks very young."

"Yes, people here age much slower."

"How do you know that you can have children? Maybe you can't be a father."

"Since they could only send so many people, we had to be tested and because I am past the normal age of marrying, I was one that got to go. It's the chance we had to take. Also, my father is an officer here and he wants grandchildren, anyway, everything was a go. All of the men lost their wives. Some of them were pregnant and they were lost also. It was a very hard thing. My father was devastated losing my mother and his only daughter. He is not pushing the ones that just lost their wives. He gave them a choice to go to Earth to choose another woman or they could wait until we went again. There were plenty of men that wanted to go on this trip."

"I'm sorry! Well now that you have lost your women, you will never be able to have a wife to live with forever. That's almost sad."

"True, but I can't help to hope that you decide to stay here."

"You know I have children and can't do that. Even if I do decide to leave John, I have to get back to my children. You did promise Miim."

"I know, and I will keep my promise, but I am human and have needs. I love the idea of being married. I just wished I would have found someone, and had a son."

"I'm sorry, maybe some other woman will stay. You are very nice looking so that shouldn't be too hard."

"Thanks, but I would not take another man's chosen one. You are my pick and my only chance for the next two years anyway. If this does not work out, I might get to go back and try again but doubtful. Time is running out for me."

"Miim, tell me about this illness. How do you know that it won't happen again?"

"Anything can happen but we are sure we found the cure. It had something to do with the genes. The reproductive cells were attacked by a virus called Irotonin. It could happen to Earth people as well because we don't know how far back this started or what caused it to become active. It's a virus that has been dormant, we think, for many generations. If this does happen again, even to Earth, we think we can help because we now know the cure, and of course that is what we would do."

"I think I'm starting to understand."

We stopped at a very large building, again round in shape. When Miim opened the door I was in awe. I looked around and there were many large round buildings and people everywhere. The buildings were lit up so much, that it appeared to be daylight outside although it was dark. Again, all the buildings were white in color.

"Are all your buildings white?" I asked.

"Yes, They show up the light better and the material comes from our mountains. Unlike your planet, we don't get as much sun or moon light as you do."

"I guess you need a lot of electricity up here, huh?"

"Yes, something like that."

"I guess those women are Earthlings," I said as he took my hand to help me from the car and told me how beautiful I looked again.

"Yes, I guess you can say that," he smiled. "I bet you thought you would never get to go shopping again," he said as he pointed to some buildings on the other side of the dining building.

"Wow, they have clothes and stuff in there?"

"Yes, and tomorrow I will take you shopping, although you look beautiful in what I picked out for you.

You will need some more clothes and personal needs. It will be fun."

"Thanks, I could never imagine John doing anything like this for me or even thinking it would be fun. Don't you do anything like work or something that you have to go to?"

"Yes, all the men pitch in and do anything that needs done, but I am on leave right now. I could not go get you and leave you on your own until you get use to being here. I have another week, and I will return to business. We don't have money like you have it. We just have these cards and we get anything we want."

"What do you do?"

"Come on, I will show you."

Miim led me to some steps. I noticed that everything looked so clean and bright. The steps in the building that we entered went on around the building. It reminded me of our capital. There were people everywhere but not a lot of women. I could not help to stare in disbelief how handsome these men were. They all seemed to be joking around with the women they were with.

"I guess the women over there are Earthlings too Miim?"

"Yes he said with a chuckle, they are from Earth. You will get a chance to meet some inside."

We walked on up the stairs, and into a very large room with a lot of people, and again a few women. Miim reached in his pocket and pulled out a plastic card and inserted it into a slot, and a light that was yellow turned red.

"This is one of the things I do," he said with a grin.

"What?"

"I am on the other side doing the accounting, not just for the dinning building but for all the buildings. It usually keeps me busy. Now watch me as we go through the line. You might have to do this on your own one day."

As we entered the large room I noticed how beautiful it was. It looked like they were about to have a New Year's party. The lighting was dim and everything looked silvery. Everyone was dressed up and some were eating and others standing around talking. They all appeared to be very happy. A lot of laughing going on. There were quite a few young boys and teenagers gathered around carrying on with each other. Even they looked like they were enjoying the women being here and waited their turn to talk to them. They were excited to find out more about Earth. I couldn't help but smile, and I felt unbelievably comfortable, and very peaceful.

"Wow, it's beautiful, is it like a party every day?"

"No," Miim said smiling down at me. "This is a special celebration to honor the Earth women."

"Wow," I said again. "I can't imagine any of our men doing this for our women."

Miim smiled again!

I followed him as he picked up food. Since I didn't recognize any of it he picked up my food also. He explained to me what everything was as he made a few suggestions. He spoke to several people as he went through the line and introduced me to his friends. He seemed very proud if me and it made me feel very comfortable.

"That's my father," he said pointing to an older gentleman talking to someone.

"What do I call him?"

"Same as I do, Sem Dioa Miim, it means the elder Miim. He is getting ready for the meeting."

"Is he like a police officer?"

"You might call it that only there is no uniform or anything. He is more like your mayor, come on we will sit with him and give him a chance to meet you."

"Oh no, what if I say something wrong, or make a fool out of myself?"

"I doubt that, come on, just be yourself. He will love you, I promise."

Miim set the food on the table and introduced me to his dad and I could tell he was his father. He had the same winning smile that women fall in love with. He was older of course but still strikingly handsome. They were the same height. Other than a few lines and graying hair, they could have been twins. I immediately liked him.

"Good evening Sam Doi Miim," I said as I was trying to remember the right way to say it. They both begin to laugh.

"What did I do?" I asked, and I know I was turning red.

"Nothing really," Miim said still laughing. "You just called my father, "The Son.""

"I knew I was not going to get that right," I said a little embarrassed. "I am so sorry sir, I mean Sem."

"Don't worry, I'm sure it will take some time to learn our customs," he said with a smile. He also told me he thought his son chose well when he chose me. I didn't know if I should be honored or mad so I kept the comments to myself.

I ate everything that Miim picked out for me. I guess I didn't realize how hungry I was. I found some foods were not unlike our own. Most was very good and I complimented on them. I guess you could say by now I was getting a little more comfortable about being here. Everyone did seem very nice, and everyone treated each other with love and respect.

"Do you have other relatives here Miim?"

"Yes, I have an uncle, his name is Sem Ranor Radge, but he is not here yet. He lost his wife also, my aunt Arine. They have a son that should be here soon. His name is Ravone, a fine young man."

"I'm sorry you lost so many people. Do you think it would be okay if I go talk to that girl over there? She appears to be confused and afraid," I asked as soon as we were finished eating, and Miim started to talk business with his father.

"Sure" they both said in unison. Just be careful, we don't want to frighten anyone. We do encourage you to make friends with the others," Miim said, almost in a whisper.

"Hi, what is your name?" I asked as I approached her.

"Krista," she answered, "were you brought up here against your will also?"

"Yes, my name is Angie and I have two children and a husband on Earth. Did someone tell you why you are here?"

"Yes his name is Ribar, he is over there." Krista pointed to a man now talking with Miim and his father. "I don't want to stay here. I need to get home to my husband and kids."

"Yea, me too, listen Krista the only thing we can do is cooperate with these guys for now. Maybe we can make them believe that we have to get back. Don't be afraid, they seem to be very nice and you have to admit Ribar is a very nice looking man. Maybe we can come up with a plan. I really don't think they mean us harm. Do you see the man Ribar is talking to? That's the one that picked me out. Looks like they are about to have a meeting, so I will try to talk to you later. Let's listen to what they have to say. Maybe we can get some answers here tonight."

"I think she will be alright," I said to Miim when I returned to our table. "She is just a bit frightened."

"Thanks, maybe we will make you a consultant to the women or something."

"How do you know that I didn't tell her that we are all going to run?"

"You didn't!"

"Oh, I forgot, you guys read minds, right?"

Miim grinned!

Miim's father stood up to a speaker and most people took seats when he asked for their attention. I found out later that it was part of their custom out of respect for the speaker.

"I suppose all of you know by now what is going on and why you are here. We want to put your mind at ease. We don't want to hurt anyone. I think you know by now that we love our women and will do anything to keep you happy and safe, but our planet is in trouble. Earth people are similar to our own people and the only ones that can help us. We do not want your planet as our enemies, so we are going to rely on the women that are here to explain and reason with your other people when you return. We do want you to be honest with them. We are asking that each of you have a girl child with our men that have selected you as possibilities. Please believe us

43

when we tell you that we could find no other way to save our planet from extinction. Now, here is our plan. In the time you are here, each of you should be able to have two children. We are hoping that most of you will have girls but we will need boys also. If you have one of each that would be good. Now, how each of you cooperate will make a difference when we can get you back home. We figure this will take about two years or maybe less. There are three hundred and ten of you. If all of you give us two children our planet will not be lost. I will take any questions now. Please give us your name so that we can get to know you."

"My name is Tammie," a pretty girl with long dark hair raised her hand. "What if we did cooperate with you and we don't have a girl, does that mean we will have to stay until we have one?"

"No it does not, Sem Diao Miim replied. "Unless it is your own decision to stay, we will not hold you once you have two children."

Another girl raised her hand and asked, why didn't they just go to Earth and tell them what they needed, and let them help them?

"Do you really think your men would cooperate with us? The men that you are staying with now have explained to you why it was necessary to choose women that have children, but what you don't know is that all of you have troubled marriages. We planned it that way because it makes it easier for you to cooperate with us and eases the pain of missing your husband. Of course in the end we would like you to stay with us. We know that you will miss your children, and that is understandable. That also lets us know that you are good mothers. All your children are school age we did not want to take a mother away from a child that is too young. If this does not work we will only have to go back to Planet Earth to repeat our attempts. Looking on our side of the problem, that would only delay trying to populate our planet not to mention a lost two years. Now unless there is more questions I would like to see all of you get to know each other, and have some fun. While you are here, and I mean this with all my heart, I hope some of you will decide that you love us, and our planet, and decide to stay with your new children. If this happens then we will find a way to get your children from Earth. Now let's just have some fun, have a little music and dance if you want to, but most of all get to know each other."

"Miim, what if we only have one child? Does that mean you will hold us until we have a second one?" I asked still not taking all of this in.

"Does that mean that you are going to cooperate with me?" he asked with a grin of satisfaction.

"Absolutely not!" I said with a bit of frown and my arms folded across my chest. He gave me another grin and winked.

I stood up and walked away from him. I did not want him to have the least bit of satisfaction of thinking he has won. I walked over to where a group of women were conversing, including Tammie and Krista. I also met Julie and Karen, each one nice looking women in their mid to late twenties. Each one pointed out the men they were with and every one of them nice looking and nicely built. Ann was even happy with the situation. She was looking for an affair after her husband of eight years had an affair. She said she was about to file for a divorce when she was kidnapped. "I plan to cooperate with him fully," she told us. She thought Derrif was so sweet and told us he knows how to treat a woman. All the girls agreed that the men that brought them here were great, but only Ann made the decision to fully cooperate. Krista seemed more relaxed, and she was dancing with Ribar. It looked like she was having a great time.

"Well I don't intend to cooperate myself," I said stubbornly. "Miim is really nice but he is sure of himself that I will, and I am not going to be his bargain chip."

"Angie," Tammy said, quite sternly, "If you don't, the rest of us would have to stay longer against our will. We have to think about this. What if our planet had the same problem? Wouldn't we do the same thing? Karn is over there looking at me. I know that he admires me and I think I'm going to go to him. I am thinking more on what Ann is thinking."

"I doubt that you would have to stay longer. I think they expect a few to refuse them. Anyway, let's plan to get together again tomorrow to discuss this further. If everyone is in agreement, I may rethink this. I just need time to think it over. I believe they are giving us time to adjust. How about after dinner tomorrow?"

I looked over to where Miim stood and noticed another man and a teenager I hadn't seen before, was talking to him. I figured it was his uncle and cousin. His uncle looked a lot like his father and the teenager looked like a younger version of Miim. I saw Miim looking around as if looking for me, so I walked over to where he was standing with Karn and the strangers. He introduced me to them as if he was proud of me.

"She's perfect!" His uncle said to Miim.

"Yes, I know," Miim said, as he looked down at me with flirting eyes. "Dance with me." He stretched out his arm toward me.

I hesitated, and I noticed most of the women were dancing, and having a good time. The temptation was great, but I was not yet ready to make this kind of move, or allow him to think that later, he can make a move on me. Luckily, his cousin was waiting to talk to me. I asked Miim if he minded if I spent some time with him. Miim seemed pleased that I took the time for him. After talking to Ravone for awhile, I thought maybe it was time to leave before Miim asked me to dance again.

"Miim do you mind if we leave? I am very tired and I just want to get some rest."

"No, of course not Honey," Miim said very sweetly. I was not convinced if it was for my benefit or his uncle's. I was just having a tough time believing all his sincerity.

"Your father, cousin and uncle are very nice," I said as we walked out the door. "So are all of your friends."

"Hey, what about me? I'm the one that has to impress you."

"You're the one that is trying to get me pregnant, remember."

"Is that such a bad thing. You did tell your husband you wanted another child."

"I didn't mean by a total stranger."

"But I won't be a total stranger for long. You can take as much time as you need. Honest Honey, I will not try to rush you, at least not for now."

"Don't call me that, I'm not your honey." I said as I stepped up my pace to walk in front of him.

"Okay, I will wait to call you that in about a week, by then we will not be strangers."

He was either making fun of me, or trying awfully hard, but I was not buying it. It only made me more furious.

"That's not funny! It appears that you have known me longer than I have known you."

"Okay, I will stop teasing. I like you a lot Angie, and I just want you to know the real me. We're not here just to make out with you. Can we at least be friends for now, please?"

"Okay friends, that's it, just friends. If I have to live in your house, I guess being friendly is better than being shackled."

He gave me another one of those winning smiles. I think he knows that his beautiful smile is what will win me over, but I will have news for this conceited guy.

"Miim, I was talking to Ravone, he is very young but by the time he is able to get married there will be no one in his age group. What happens to the teenagers here?"

"The only plan we have for now is take him to Earth when he gets a little older. It could be that the children of the women that are already here will come back here. We think after you get to know us, most will want to live here. That way the gap will be filled."

"Wow, this is some plan you guys have."

The next day we went shopping for clothes and a few other needs. We had so much fun. I don't remember laughing so much, and never did John and I have this much fun. He didn't even like shopping with me. Miim wanted to buy me everything and he clapped every time

I tried something on. I couldn't help getting silly. After buying a few personal needs, we went to the large dining hall. I saw a few women but only one I recognized. Tammie and Karn were sitting together, laughing and having a good time. They looked like they belonged together. They looked up long enough to wave, and then they were back into each other. *Am I the only one that is not cooperating with these men*? I thought.

"Let me take you for a walk after we eat," Miim said, "I want to show you something."

"Okay, just don't call it a date. This place sure looks different from yesterday. I'm sorry we left early. I know your men went to a lot of trouble to make us feel comfortable and show us a good time. I do appreciate what they did."

"Everyday is a date for us. That's why we are a contented people. You don't have to be sorry, I understand how you feel. I just want to take you somewhere that I know you will like. Come on, it will be fun."

"Not because you want me to cooperate with you?"

"Now would I have come up with something like that on my own?" Miim asked teasingly.

"Never," I teased back throwing a piece of my napkin at him.

A couple of the other girls walked in and I had a chance to talk to them. I found out that Krista had two little girls at home but her husband was abusive. She was afraid of staying away because she didn't know what he would do to her when she got back. At least he was good to the kids. Ann had three children, a daughter and twin boys. She told us that her husband didn't even want children after they were already married and now he spends more time away so that he doesn't have to deal with them. We offered pictures to each other and had some talk time.

"Are you ready to go?" Miim asked, "I want you to see this by daylight and then after it turns dark."

We walked about two blocks to what I thought was a very nice park. It had odd color rocks lined up near a bridge over a pond. Most were pink, reds and blues. Flowers blended with the rock colors. Some places it was hard to tell what was flowers and what was rocks. Everywhere there was beauty like I had never seen before. It reminded me of a cottage picture in one of those paintings, almost unreal.

"This is beautiful, Miim," I said with excitement.

"I knew you would like it," he said as he was taking in the beauty himself. "I try to walk here every day. I can never get tired of it." He seemed to enjoy my excitement.

We walked around until it got dark and we sat on a bench, where colored lights showed upon the pond. It was breathtakingly beautiful. "I've never seen so much beauty," I said as I turned to him smiling.

"I agree" he said as he looked down at me, serious, wanting, caring.

"This hasn't changed anything Miim, and I'm not beautiful."

"You are beautiful, and I can't help the way I feel."

"Miim, you are very sweet and I can see where people could fall in love with this place it is so perfect but I need to know where I stand with John. I just can't turn off our marriage like it never existed."

"I understand Angie" He looked at me, and I could see the deep hurt in his eyes. I could also see that he had feelings for me. He also knew that I was not ready to give up on my marriage vows. I told him this, and he told me that the marriage vows were broken the day that John cheated on me. I knew he was right, but I still had to know why John did what he did. I had to figure out what went wrong with our marriage.

"Come on, let's go home, Angie. Take my hand, the rocks here are a bid unsteady and I can't have you hurt."

I took his hand and I was upset with myself to feel how comfortable it felt.

CHAPTER FOUR

Carrie listened as I told her every detail. "It sounds like a ferry tale or more like you were living in a fantasy world," she said, somewhat believing me. "I've got a feeling there is a lot more."

"Yes there is. I just don't know what I want to do. John cheated on me, and I don't know if I can stay with him or trust him again. Carrie I have to find out what my feelings are for him. Right now, I am so confused and hurt. I guess I will have to find out what my marriage is all about because within the next couple months I have to make a decision that will affect the rest of our lives, including the children."

The phone rang, and as I got up to answer it, Carrie made a comment. "Why do I have a feeling that something bad is about to happen?" I wondered what she meant as I walked over to pick up the phone.

"Angie, I need to talk to you now," Grant sounded urgent.

"Do you want to come over here?"

"No, I don't want John to hear this. I have a feeling you're not telling me everything. We have some more information that I need to confirm. I think you will talk more freely when John is not around. He wanted me to call him before I talk to you again and he will be mad, but that's tough."

"Okay, I'll be there, give me about half and hour."

"See you in a bit."

"Carrie, I have to go. Grant wants to talk to me without John being there. I will call you when I get away from him. Can you drop me off on your way home?"

"Of course, do you want me to go with you?"

"No, this could take awhile."

"Promise me you will call the very minute you get home."

"I will, unless John is there. I have to tell you everything. If it's not too late, I will stop by on my way home."

"Come in, shut the door," Grant said, as he stopped some paper work and threw his pencil on his desk. "Do you know a woman named Tammie Brenson?"

"Yes, she is one of the other women that got captured."

"Well she is telling us that she was forced to stay on that planet Cribaar until she had two children by one of the aliens. Is this true?"

"Yes!"

"Also, they are here again steeling our women so that they can rape them and then send them back to us only to get more women. When is this suppose to stop? What is going on here? I want to hear this in your own words, and this time don't leave anything out." Grant was angry with me but I told him that I could not talk freely in front of John. He pointed to a chair for me to sit.

"Grant it wasn't like that. They did not rape the women. They just made it easier to leave if we cooperated with them. Put yourself in their shoes. They were about to lose their planet because all their women died. I guess you can say they had to replenish."

"Damn it Angie, do you actually think they can do this and get away with it? This is bigger than I am. I will have to call in higher authorities."

"Do you think they will believe you? I guess you have to do what you have to do, but I don't agree. I will tell you everything Grant, from the beginning. I did try to talk to you and John, but what I did tell you, you didn't believe me. I felt like both of you were laughing at me."

"I believe you, but John called me after he got to work and told me that you were making this story up just so you wouldn't look bad. He can't explain the other women that were missing but he thinks you had an affair." His voice was much more calm as he went on.

"John is angry with me because we accused him of doing something to you. Now he is talking about suing the damn police department. Tammie is here Angie. Let me get her, and I want to talk to you together. Tammie, it seems, wants to go back to that planet. We can't allow that Angie, you have to know that. It would start some kind of panic. All of this has to go away. I can not allow you or her to leave with these men. Did you plan to go back with them? Tell me now Angie."

"How can you tell us what to do? These men are so sweet, they don't want to harm us. They are so kind and gentle. The choices they made were a must because they were dying off. We have to have some compassion for them Grant. If we needed the help they need now, they would help us."

Tammie and I were in Grant's office for over two hours telling him everything that we could remember, verifying each others stories. He also wanted to know where they were now, but we told him they thought it was best that we didn't know. Both of us knew how to get in touch with them if we needed to, but neither of us told him that part. I did tell him a lot more than I told John.

"That is all that I remember Grant, down to every detail."

"This is some story, it sounds like a science fiction novel."

"We know Sgt. Wayne. In the beginning that is what we thought," Tammie said, with all sincerity. We learned that these people are regular people but more compassion for each other than we have for our own people. How can this go wrong? We automatically assume they are enemies because they live on another planet. Sgt. Wayne, these people are not our enemies. They our us. Killing them would be like killing our own innocent people."

"Tammie, you can not go to this guy. I can not allow you to do this. If this causes a panic, we would have to have a full investigation. It would not only put these aliens in danger but it would also put us in danger. I can't tell you what's going to happen. If they are found, our military may even wipe them out. You know how they are. They will act out of fear and protection for all of us. Don't you see what could happen here? They don't know these aliens are good people. I want both of you to stay put until I can get some information on my next move."

Tammie and I looked at each other in disbelief. When Grant got up, turned around to put our file away, we both silently and slowly shook our head, no. I think we both were thinking the same thing, and thank God, I got her telephone number before we got back to Earth. We have to warn them.

"Grant," I turned around to face him as I was about to walk out the door. "Did you know before I went missing that John was cheating on me, or am I the only stupid fool around?"

"We found out while you were gone, that's one of the reasons that he was under suspicion. How did you find out?"

"Miim told me and he had pictures. Thanks for being honest with me."

"Sounds like these people know more about us than we do them, kind of creepy. Angie, listen, if you want to talk, I mean on the personal level, let me know. You and I have been more friends than John and I have been."

"Thanks," I said again. "Grant these people are far more advanced than we are and Miim told me that their ancestors came from Earth. I don't know how they ended up on another planet and I'm not sure they know. I think the secret to that died long ago. I just know that they are good people, not looking for trouble. They originally went there to find peace and perfection. They are God's people and I don't think we should harm them. I'm asking you to let this go."

Grant remained silent but I knew he considered what I was saying.

I caught up with Tammie. She assured me that she would notify the men at the spaceship to let them know what Grant told us. We were able to compare notes and decided we would lie if it meant keeping them safe. Tammie thought it didn't seem to matter to Grant that we believe these men are harmless.

It was too late to go over to Carrie's after staying at Grant's office for several hours. I called her to let her know that I would see her Monday. I wanted to get home before John got home.

John got in earlier than he promised, and brought in some dinner for us. Pleased with himself, he held a large bag up shaking it, letting me know that it was one of my favorites. He walked up to me and kissed me a quick kiss like I never did go missing for so long.

"Are you ready to be honest with me?" he asked, as he pulled out a couple of plates and forks.

"That's a strange choice of words, honest," I repeated after him.

"What's that suppose to mean, Angie?"

"It means yes, before the children come home, we do need to be honest with each other."

"What do you mean honest with each other? I'm not the one that took off, to God knows where and stayed away for almost three years." He had a disgusted look on his face. A deep frown that covered his whole face when he became angry with me. I think he used it when he wanted me to back off or when I said something he did not want to hear.

"True, but you are partly to blame."

"Angie, don't make it look like my fault, you left me remember?"

"Not by my own free will," I corrected. "Have you been seeing Kay, John?" I asked, only now he knew the anger was rising up in me. He stood looking at me silent, like he was planning his next words carefully, and there it was again. He thrust his hands deeply into his pockets and jingled his change. He was nervous as hell, and he knew I had him over a barrel.

"I see Kay every day, she works for me remember."

"I think you know what I mean."

"Well what the hell did you expect me to do Angie? You disappear for two and a half years. I thought you were dead, so yes, Kay and I have been seeing each other. Now that you are back I will call it off."

"Well that answered my next question. I meant before I left, while you were sleeping with me. Were you sleeping with Kay then?"

"Where the hell did you get that information?"

"Pictures, here, I have them right here." I was proud of myself for being so calm as I handed them to John.

Johns eyes got larger as he looked at the pictures. He had the look as if he got his hands caught in a cookie jar.

"Where did you get these? You had me followed didn't you? All this time you never trusted me, and you were watching me make a mistake so that you could run off with that other man."

"What difference does it make John, you cheated on me even while I was home. Don't make it my fault. You were not even completely honest with me until you saw these pictures." I was even more angry then before and I knew at that point I could never stay with him. "Now

I will tell you the story you have been waiting to hear, but nothing will ever be good between us again. It's true that I was captured by aliens and held against my will. At first I was terrified, but when I found out how sweet they were, I begin to trust them. I had no intentions of falling in love with one of them until I saw the pictures of you and Kay. It still took me a while but I finally gave in and had his child. Yes John, I have another child by an alien."

John and I talked until almost midnight, I told him almost everything that I remembered, whether he believed me or not, I don't know. It didn't matter. I made up my mind what I was going to do. I just didn't want to tell him what I planned to do next. I didn't want him to stop me. He kept looking at me in disgust, and every once in a while I reminded him of his infidelity. Several times he got up and paced the floor, and he would thrust his hands in his pockets, jingling his change. He was angry with me, but I was just as angry. Only difference was, he was not use to my speaking back to him in this manner.

"What about the children?" he asked. "You can't take the children away from me."

"I don't know John, we will have to work this out." I walked out, not looking back. I didn't feel anything for him.

"I will not make this easy for you Angie," he yelled at me as I walked away. He stood up again, and I thought he would come after me, but he decided to sit down again. I figured he was thinking about his next move. I stayed in the guest room that night, now I had a good reason to. I locked the door for fear that he would come in after me. I knew he would start drinking and would not be in a good mood. He might even get aggressive. I listened out for him, but he must have gone on to bed. I did not hear any more from him that night.

The next day John and I went to see Andrew and Alyssa. We didn't say much to each other on the four hour drive it took to my parent's, except to say we would not tell the kids about our problems yet. We agreed only to tell them parts of what happened to me, and leave out the alien part. We did not want them to think everything was going to be alright, when later we would have to tell them we will not be together. We also decided to leave the children with my parents until summer break in a few weeks. I knew the children would not be happy about it, but it would give us time to take care of some things, including a divorce, although that was not discussed yet.

As we approached my parents farm, I was getting very nervous about seeing the children. Will they still love me as much as I love them? Would they even remember me? Alyssa was very young when I disappeared.

"Alyssa, Honey, look at you, you're all grown up," I cried as I took my sweet daughter in my arms. "I didn't think you were going to remember me."

Alyssa resembled me more than she did John. She had the same color of hair and eyes and thin face that I have, but she did have John's smile. She has grown so much. Right now she just giggled that same sweet giggle that I remembered. I cried as I held her. I never want to be away from my children again.

"I have your picture, Mommy. I always keep it beside my bed, and I pray for you everyday. I ask God to bring you back to us."

"Oh Honey, thank you for not giving up on me. I missed you so much, and we have so much to talk about."

"What happened to you Mommy, why couldn't you come home?"

"Honey, I promise I will tell you, but right now let's go see Andrew. Where is he?"

"He is down at the barn. He cleans the barn on Saturdays."

"Okay, let's you and I go see him."

Andrew threw himself at me and cried so hard that I couldn't help from letting my tears go. I thought he would never stop crying. Andrew has always been the more sensitive one. I guess that's where he takes after me.

"Mom, please don't leave us again," he sobbed.

"Andrew, what is it? Are you okay? I'm here now sweetheart."

"Yea Mom, I just missed you. I didn't think you were ever going to come home. I thought you were dead. I love you Mom." He held on to me very tightly.

"Oh Honey, I love you too. You know I would not leave you for so long if I had a choice, don't you?"

"You tell me who did this to you, and I will get them."

"I will tell you and your sister all about it, but for now, you finish your chores. I will go see your grandparents so they can see that I am okay. How has your grandparents been treating you?"

"Good, I just have to stay busy so I can keep out of trouble," he said, as he walked back to his work.

"Listen, you finish up your work and I'll be back to get you. Andrew, everything is going to be okay."

Alyssa and I walked back to the small farm house. The children loved coming here when they were small. They liked feeding and petting the animals and catching tadpoles down by the stream. Their dad and grandfather took them to the lake to go swimming and fishing. As I looked around, I thought this would have been a great place for children to grow up, but my father drank heavy back then. It carried some bad memories for me. My father was more abusive towards my older brothers, Adam and Bret. They had little time for themselves. They had so many chores to do. When my father would drink, usually on week-ends, he would tell them they were not worth anything except to be horse farmers. They could never seem to do anything right, and he was always on their backs. Sometimes he would beat them if they did not do things as he expected. My brothers were afraid of him, and one time I overheard Adam say he was going to kill him. I remember spending the next couple of weeks thinking my father would be dead at anytime. Dad did not beat me, but he pushed me out of his way when I would try to talk to him. He told me on several occasions that I was stupid. He does not drink anymore because of health problems. He is easier to get along with. I still could not find myself talking to him, and I avoided him whenever I could. He gets along with John better than he does with me or his own sons. My parents have always liked John, even when John used to come over to spend time with me when we were teens. They both wanted me to marry him, and we married at a very early age. I thought I was in love with him but now I wonder if I just wanted an out.

"Angie," Mom came out on the porch to greet me. "I am so glad that you are okay, we all have been so worried about you." She hugged me and kissed me on the cheek.

"I'm okay Mom, don't worry," I said as I hugged her back. She is a tall lady and still attractive for her age except she has put on a little extra weight and her hair has gotten grayer. I got along with her okay but I felt she never defended us against my father when he drank and got mean. She would always make excuses for his behavior. I knew Mom loved us, but she was not very affectionate. I was very lonely as a child. My brothers were four and five years older than I, so I did not play with them much. I only had the animals to play with. When I was older, she didn't do the things with me that mother and daughters do. I did have a lot of chores to do when the boys were gone, but she didn't have much to talk to me about.

As we walked in the house, our, backs against Alyssa, Mom said in a low voice, "John tells me that you are getting a divorce."

"Boy he didn't waste any time. He could have waited until I could talk to you myself. We didn't talk about a divorce, but I guess he can correctly assume that it is a possibility."

"You have to consider the kids Angie, what ever the problem, I'm sure you can work it out."

"Did he tell you why?"

"Angie, he thought you were gone forever, we all did," Mom said in a louder voice, I thought was not necessary. "John is a wonderful guy, you will not do any better. I think you should stay married to him. The kids need him."

"Obviously he neglected to tell you that he was cheating on me while I was home."

"Is that why you left?" she asked sternly. Her voice was getting loud and gruff.

"Alyssa, go tell your brother that I want to take you two for a walk after dinner."

After Alyssa was gone, I turned around to my mother. "Please don't talk like this in front of the children. I'm sure they are confused enough, and I don't want them to overhear what we are saying. Mom we haven't talked to them yet. We don't know what we are going to do ourselves, and John should not have told you anything until we do decide."

"Your children should know what you are doing to their father Angie."

"Mom," I snapped. "We need a chance to talk to the children ourselves. You only heard Johns side and it sounds like he sugar coated what he has been doing. He cheated on me and lied about it, and no, that is not the reason I left. I was kidnapped, Mother. I guess I had better get in here and see Dad. We will talk about this when the children go to bed."

Dad and John were in the small living room talking and smoking. Dad stood up, gave me a hug, but did not say anything. He sat down and resumed his conversation with John. It didn't surprise me that my father didn't have much to say to me. I looked at him noticing he hasn't changed much either. He has aged a lot, but that was probably from his drinking catching up with him. He looked much older than Mom, but there was only three years difference. He is small framed for a man and very thin. Mother stands a little taller than he does.

He is the one I take after in looks and build. I looked around the room, and noticed things looked the same as I remembered, even as I was growing up. Same color walls, same curtains and decorations, and even the same furniture although a bit worn by now. I figured I was not wanted on this conversation, so I decided to go back to talk to Mom and get it over with. I couldn't help wondering why my father hated me so much. I'm sure he blames me for my wanting to leave John, but than again, I don't ever remember him giving me any kind words.

"Well I guess I will go on out and help mom with dinner," I announced, but still no activity from John or my father. *Just like him to play on their sympathy, and making me look like the bad guy,* I thought.

"Listen Angie," my mother said, again, I thought in a voice that was unnecessary, "sometimes a woman has to endure things she does not like, but for the sake of the children, they have to stay married."

"No Mom, there are no rules to say that I have to stay married. The children will know that we are having problems and it will only be harder on them. Did dad ever cheat on you Mom?"

"Not that I know of, but I guess it wouldn't surprise me if I found out he did. I just never did try to find out. It wouldn't have changed anything." She set the glasses down that she got down from the cabinet and paused. Her back was to me. She was speaking slowly, somberly, like she knew something that she didn't want me to know. She was hurting!

"Would you have stayed with him if you knew he had?"

"Of course I would have. Where else would I have gone? I had three kids to take care of, and I loved your father."

"Mom do you realize at all how unhappy your three kids were? For that matter, how unhappy you were?" I walked over to stand in front of her. I watched her expression. She looked tired, unhappy and about to cry.

"I guess you were like any other kids." She said slowly, head hanging down.

"No, we were not like any other kids. Our father drank and beat my brothers and he was mean to all of us, including you. I hated my life. I couldn't wait to get out of here. Don't you see that's why I got married at such an early age. I don't think I was really ever in love with John. I was with him because that's what everyone else wanted me to do. At the time, I thought he offered me a better life. Is this the kind of life you want for your grandchildren? Mom get this, I am in love with another man. I found out what true love is all about while I was gone. At first I was kidnapped but he treated me with love and respect. I do not intend to spend the rest of my life with a cheating, uncaring husband."

"Now Angie, things were not all that bad." She continued to get plates from the cabinet, and handed them to me. "Your father is a very sick man and I want you to try to make things right with him. He probably only has a year or so to live."

"I didn't know! Just now when I went in to see him, he just gave me a short hug, and didn't say one word. I feel like I disgust him."

"Just give him a chance, he will come around. He has been having a great time with his grandchildren and I think they love him. Come on now, let's put the finishing touches on this dinner and we will get everyone together. It will be like old times."

Funny not one word about how I am, and what I was going through. Most of the concern seemed to be for John.

"Adam is coming over later to see you. He is getting married in a few months you know."

"No I didn't know, I am so happy for him."

I couldn't wait to see my older brother. I didn't think he would ever get married. He seemed like such a loner and very shy. When we were growing up together the three of us were very close. Sometimes we would plot to run away, although, we never did. Adam was the one that would watch over me and protect me from danger. When we got a little older we would talk for hours into the night. We had no television or games. We just liked each other's company. I always thought of him as my hero.

I went down again to the barn to let the children know that dinner was ready. They were talking, teasing and laughing. It was so great to be with my children again, and hear their laughter.

"Hi Mom," Andrew said with a grin.

"Hi Andrew, come on you guys I will race you to the house, it's dinner time." We laughed and ran all the way back.

Except for the children chatting away, dinner time was very quiet. Every once in a while Andrew would reach over and touch me as if to see if I was real and I might disappear if he didn't. I just smiled at him and I would touch him back, thinking how tough all this has been on him.

After dinner, Alyssa helped her grandma with dishes and I went out to the porch with Dad, John and Andrew.

"Andrew, your dad and I would like it if you would stay here and finish school."

"But Mom, you said you wanted us home and we could come home with you now."

"Andrew," John scolded, "we are not giving you a choice. You will stay here until school year is out."

Andrew walked on into the house, very upset, but did not say a word. I followed him in and put a hand on his shoulder. "Come on I will tell you some things about what happened to me. Want to walk?"

"No, I'm tired."

"Okay, let's just go to your room. I will talk to Alyssa later."

I told him how I was captured but did not give him many details. I just wanted to give him time to adjust. The main thing was to let him know that I would never have left him if I had a choice.

"I'm sorry we can't take you home now. Mom & Dad need to fix some things, and we will be back to get you. You believe me don't you?"

"Sure Mom! Did those men hurt you?" he asked. He was the only one besides Grant and Carrie that were concerned enough to ask.

"No Honey, they were actually very kind. They had reasons to take me, and I will explain it all to you one day. For now I want you to be okay. I will be back for you soon. It's only a few weeks until school is out and then we will spend the summer together. I don't want to be away from you one second more than I have to," I told him as I gave him a hug.

"Okay Mom, after I get a shower I'm going to play a game and go to bed. I'll see you in the morning. I love you Mom." He said this while waving to me. He was smiling.

"I love you too sweetheart. Don't forget to brush your teeth. I will see you in the morning too." I waved and smiled back.

After I put Alyssa to bed and read her a story I came back to the porch to talk to my parents again. I was not sure what to say, but I needed to break the ice with my dad and then try to explain to them what happened to me.

"Dad, Mom told me that you have not been well."

"Yep, I guess drinking finally caught up with me. I guess I have a year or two."

"I'm sorry, are you sure you are up to keeping the kids longer."

"Yep, they've been company to me, and Andy has been helping me with the chores."

"Listen both of you. I know that you don't believe that John and I should get a divorce, but I can't live with him knowing he has cheated on me, even before I was captured. He lied when I asked him about it." I looked over at John and he just looked away from me with a hurt look on his face. I figured he was gaining sympathy from my parents.

"You got to think of your kids Angie," Dad said looking down to the ground, as he was swinging slowly back and forth.

"I am Dad. You and I both know that I was not happy as a child. I want better for my kids. Doesn't anyone care that I was kidnapped? Only my young son asked me if I was okay. I get the picture that everyone is so worried about what might happen to John, they forget what happened to me."

About that time Adam pulled in, and hopped out of his car. I ran to him and he hugged me so hard that he lifted me clean off my feet. Adam had hair and eyes like mine, but took after Mom on his height and build. He is larger built than Bret. I guess that is why I thought of him as my hero. He is very good looking and has a sweet personality.

"You just saved me from getting very mad at Dad," I said. "Oh Adam, I missed you so much."

"I've missed you too Ange." He squeezed my shoulders again, as we walked back to the porch.

Adam and Bret, are the only ones that called me Ange, and boy did it ever sound good.

"Come on let's go up to the porch. Mom tells me you're getting married. I want to know all about her and your wedding. I'm so excited for you."

"You will love her, Ange. She is so much like you, sweet and affectionate. Her name is Julie. Sorry she can't be here now. She's still finishing up some college courses."

"I love her already. I hope I can meet her before the wedding. What about Bret, how is he doing?"

"He's about the same, still living out west. I called to tell him that you're back. He and Sue are still happily married and Joanie their youngest is as cute as a button."

"Thanks Adam, I hope to get out to see them. I have never seen Joanie. What is she, almost four?"

"Yes, and Teddy is six. I'm sure they will be in for the wedding."

"I hope so, it will be great to see them."

By the time Adam and I got back to the porch, everyone's conversation took another direction. At least my divorce can be forgotten for awhile.

"I want to hear about your wedding Adam," I said, "and don't leave anything out."

"Well I will be getting married in July and Alyssa is going to be the flower girl and Andrew will be my best man. We will get married in the church in town that we went to as kids. As far as other details go, we have not had a chance to plan yet, but we will be doing that the next couple of months. Come on Ange, let's go for a walk. I want to hear all about where you've been."

Adam and I talked for the next hour about Julie and his up coming wedding. We also talked about my experiences, leaving out the men being aliens. I then told him that I was getting a divorce. He told me that he was not surprised, and he never thought John was good enough for me. He never cared very much for John and he didn't like his demands on me. I felt so much better that he was taking my side on this. He also told me that he would support me in any way that he could. Adam left about another hour later and I promised that I would be at his wedding.

We talked briefly to my parents, about my being captured, and nobody asked questions so we talked about other things that happened while I was gone. I don't think they believe that I was taken against my will anyway. It's hard to tell what John told them while I was walking with Adam.

Mother and I walked into the house and left my dad and John talking about some hunting experiences. Mom told me that John and I would have to sleep together because we only have the sofa bed left. I figured I would have to endure it to keep peace, but I believe she was thinking there was a chance that we would make up. I went on to bed and John came in about a half hour later. He sat on the bed beside me and told me that he didn't want to let me go, and he would do anything he had to do to keep me. "I am sorry Angie, I know I messed up and I want to make things up to you, if you just give me the chance. I love you so much."

"Why didn't you think of that when you were sleeping with Kay?" I asked gruffly.

"Honey, I made a mistake, I want to make it up to you."

"Is that what you guys call it when you cheat on your wives, a mistake?" I propped my head up with my hand and looked at him. "John, I never did anything to deserve your cheating. I was always a good wife to you, and made love with you whenever you wanted. I loved you, and would have done anything for you." I cried and then I really cried tears pouring out.

"Come on Honey, let me hold you." he said as he reached for me. I turned away from him. I couldn't even think of him touching me.

"No thank you," I said, sniffling, "Right now I just want to sleep. We can talk on the way home tomorrow."

He was not use to my refusing him, and I could since his anger. A few minutes later, he came and lay beside me.

"I'm sorry, I'm not good at trying to make up with you, but I am trying here."

"I need time to think this through. Ignoring this is not going to make it go away."

"I know, I'm sorry. What I don't understand is, before you took off, you didn't know that I was sleeping with Kay. Why did you leave?

"Obviously, you think it was my choice. I am trying to tell you I was kidnapped."

"I'm sorry," he said again.

I wondered if he really was, but it was a first, he never use to apologize to me.

I could feel him cuddling up to me during the night, and I knew he wanted me, but I couldn't wait until this night was over. I tried to move over but there was no room. I just had to endure him being very close to me.

The next day, we said good-by to the children. We assured them again that we would be getting them as soon as school was out.

The first half hour John and I were silent. I figured he might be waiting for me to start the conversation, but I was going to be just as stubborn. I felt like a new me and I was beginning to like myself. John was wrong and I was not going to give him a chance to make things right. I knew that I could never love him. I probably could have forgiven him but he lied about being with Kay before I was missing. I knew the trust was completely gone.

As we were going down a steep hill, he said, "You know I could just crash into those trees down there and we could just end all our problems."

"John," I said, in shock, remembering he did have a couple of beers before we left. "We have two children, how

Linda Schell Moats

could you do that to them? How could you even think it?"
He shifted in his seat. My God, what is he up to?

"Well at least you wouldn't be able to take the children
away from me." He shifted again.

"Do I need to bail out of here?" I said as I reached for
the door handle. I never felt more like I was married to a
stranger. "John why are you making this my fault?"

"I didn't say it was your fault. I just don't think I can
live without you and the kids." I saw tears in his eyes. I
felt fear.

"Listen John, killing us both is not the answer. We
haven't had a chance to talk things through. I haven't
made any decisions what I plan to do yet. I'm hurt! I
can't think when I'm this hurt." I knew that I was lying. I
knew exactly what I was going to do but at this moment I
had to pacify him. "Just give me some time so I can figure
things out. Tell me about Kay. Why did you think it was
necessary to cheat on me? I just want to understand."
Really, I didn't care at this point. I just needed to keep
him talking and his mind occupied.

"Kay means nothing to me. She just came on to me.
It was just sex, nothing more. All the other men at the
office are screwing around with her."

"And that makes it right?"

"No, you are a wonderful woman Angie. She doesn't
light a candle to you. She's just sexy and that's all."

"I guess you never thought I was sexy."

"I think you are."

"But not as sexy as Kay?"

"That's not the point."

"I'm trying to understand John. Was I getting
boring?"

"You're putting words in my mouth." He was speeding, but at least for now he was not threatening to run into trees.

"I'm trying to give this a reason."

"It's not that you were boring. I guess it's more like adding some extra spice in my life. Like keeping up with the times, you know, having my cake and eating it to, or something like that." He had a guilty look on his face, but it did not keep him from glancing over to me.

"I would never have done that to you. You understand what this does to my trust for you?"

"I understand and I'm sorry. I'm going to do everything I can to make you trust me again. I will never let anything or anyone come between us again. I promise you that." He had tears in his eyes. Were they real? He sounded like he was making threats like I dare you to run away again.

"You want my trust, and you just threatened to kill us both."

"Only if you try to take the kids."

Again, it sounded like he was threatening me. Only he could apologize for his behavior and threaten me at the same time. Does he think this is going to make me feel better about him? I figured there was no use talking anymore. From that point on I became afraid of him, and believed he would kill me if I left him or took the children away from him.

CHAPTER FIVE

"Carrie, I have to see you," I called her as soon as John was out of sight and I was able to call a cab. "John is acting strange and yesterday he threaten to kill us both."

"Come on over," she said anxiously.

As soon as I got there and we got comfortable in a chair outside, I told her what had happened on the way home from my parents.

"I don't like it Angie. You know that you can't trust him after what he did to you."

"As soon as we got home he went on up to bed without saying a word. This morning he just talked on and on. He acted like nothing happened. He told me that he loved me and promised he would never hurt me again. He said he realized he made a mistake and he would make it up to me. I don't know if I can ever trust him again, Carrie. I don't know what to do. I think I would have felt better if he said he was sorry for threatening our lives. One minute, he acts genuine, when he says he's sorry, and the next sentence he will kill me if I leave him."

"You don't think John would really kill you do you?"

"I don't know Carrie, I really don't think so, but I have never seen him act so strange. If anything ever happens to me you need to tell Grant about that incident."

"Please get out now Angie. Don't give him a chance to hurt you."

"I've got to stay for now and pacify him. I have to get a divorce and have a plan to get the kids."

"What did you tell John about your adventures out of earth."

"I told him everything, except a few details I thought I had better leave out, at least for now. I'm in love with Miim, and I told him that, but I don't think he believed me. He thinks I said it because I found out about his cheating on me."

"Angie I'm going to get us some coffee and then I want to hear the rest of the story, about these aliens."

"Okay," I said as soon as she got back, and we got comfortable. "Where did I leave off?"

"Where you and Miim went to that neat park."

"After we got home from the park that night, I asked Miim if he would tell me about the rest of his family."

"My mother was very special," he said, with tears welling up in his eyes. "She was so beautiful, I think she is where I got my good looks," he smiled that cute devilish smile.

"Cute," I couldn't resist teasing him.

"We were a very close family. My mother's name was Karis. She was very knowledgeable, and she was the one that would give advise to other women. She would help them with their problems. She was also a Doctor's assistant, and helped wherever necessary. She would help women who were pregnant for the first time, and helped with their infants after birth. Danime, my sister, was only fifteen when she died." He put his head down in his hands and was quiet for a minute.

"She was so sweet and beautiful. She had so much going for her and she loved life. I can't believe they are both gone." He cried, and his voice was gruff and somber.

"I'm sorry, I shouldn't have brought this up, I'm sorry." I really felt terrible.

When he didn't look up, I went over to him and laid my hand on his shoulder. "I'm sorry," I said for the third time. I was really beginning to feel bad, when he looked up at me.

"No, none of this is your fault. It's just that it has been a long time since I've allowed myself to think about it. I miss them terribly. Please don't blame yourself. It's just that Danime didn't have a chance to grow up. There were so many young girls that didn't have that chance. Some were my cousins and friends.

I allowed him to put his arms around me while tears were flowing and he seemed so sad. This man was grieving terribly bad. After a few minutes I drew back and said. "Hey, you need to give yourself time to grieve. That was a terrible loss, losing both your mother, and your sister a few months later."

"My mother died first, and almost five months later Danime died. We like to get over these things fast, because it effects our work, and others if we grieve too long. We have to look at grieving like a process of life, and not a death experience, yes?

"No Miim, that's not right, it takes some people longer to get over things like this than it does others. We can't help missing the ones we love."

"Thanks, I guess I needed to hear that. Please don't tell my father this happened. He would be truly upset with me."

"Of course I won't Miim, but he can't control how you feel. You need time and if you want to talk about them, then talk to me. I understand what you are going through. Sometimes it is good to talk about things. Most men I know keep a lot to themselves. They were brought up believing that men are not suppose to cry. That could be why they carry around so much anger. God gave us all these emotions and we should use them but it is up to us to keep them under control."

"You are special Angie, I wished I could have met you under different circumstances. You understand when we love somebody it is very deep. You are so beautiful and so sweet." He looked in my eyes with that special tenderness and affection. I knew I had to change the subject.

"I am far from beautiful. Tell me about some of your customs."

"Well they are not much different than your customs. We do have more moral standards. Everyone is treated equal. We are not without problems, but nothing big, until this disease came along. Before the disease there was no living in sin. We had to be married so it is very important to choose the one you want for your life partner. There is no divorce here and that is because we treat each other with love and respect. We all work together to treat each other as friends. We all love each other."

"I can see that. Tell me about the wedding ceremony."

"It isn't called wedding ceremony, it's a holy matrimony. Couples here will swear before God that it is a lifetime commitment. A couple will fall in love, and usually, within three months they will know if they want to be together forever. They have a pre matrimonial party and if there is anyone against their marriage they need to have a meeting with our council to figure out anything that is standing in the way. Everyone that comes has a right to agree or disagree. Usually within the next three days, they will be married. It can be delayed, or denied depending on the agreement. Then the man and woman will take vows almost like yours, only here, they take them very seriously. If they have problems, they go before our council. They help them work things out."

"Such a perfect world to live in."

"I wouldn't say perfect, but we all love it here and we love each other. We are happy."

"And when someone dies do you have funerals?"

"Yes, something like that. They are similar to your's, but we have no burial grounds. We have one large tomb. I will take you someday."

"Hey look, what do you have to eat around here? I'm getting a little hungry after that long walk in the park. Do you have some of that fruit stuff you gave me to eat when I first got here?"

"I can do better than that," he said as he got up to go into another room.

"I'm going with you so I can learn where this stuff is."

He smiled, "Thanks, you are very understanding. John does not deserve you." He put his hand on my arm as we walked to another room where he kept the snacks.

Miim and I talked late that night. I learned so much about him and his people. We talked about his planet again, and all the places he wanted to show me and people he wanted me to meet. I was actually starting to feel comfortable and safe here. I wanted to share this place with all my friends because I felt so good.

"I thought about you Carrie, and how much fun we could have. It was almost like escaping from all my problems for awhile, like living in a dream world. Except for missing you and my children, I wanted to stay for awhile."

Every day we went to the large dining hall, and some days while Miim was working, I would meet him for lunch, and then meet with some of the other girls that were there. We would go shopping, or to the game mall, and sometimes the park. We all were getting to be good friends. We found ourselves enjoying being there. Every one of the women said they have never been happier in their lives. I hated to admit, I was feeling the same way."

One day Tammie and I were walking in the park and she asked me if I have been cooperating with Miim. When I told her no, and still not planning to, she told me she thought she was pregnant.

"Well if this is what you want then go for it, but I still need to be in love, and married to the man I plan to have a child with. It's only been a few weeks, and yes, Miim has been wonderful, sexy and sweet. I still have a husband that I need to find out what his feelings are for me, and mine for him. I'm afraid I would never get my children back if I sleep with another man. I'm just not ready for another relationship, or make any kind of commitment."

"It was okay when your husband cheated on you, why not cheat on him?"

"You're beginning to sound like Miim. It's just that I have to know the reason he cheated. I need to end my relationship with my husband, and make sure I can get my children. I have to have a plan before I start a new relationship. What if John did not cheat on me? What if this is a big mistake? I can't be with Miim knowing that things at home are not resolved. Miim is not pushing me, and I respect him for it. For now let's leave it at that."

"Miim is in love with you, you know that don't you?"

"Tammie, he has not told me that. I know he has feelings for me, but the only reason I am here is because he wants a child. I need more than that from the man I plan to be with the rest of my life."

"I overheard him tell his father that he is falling hard for you."

"Miim is wonderful, and I have feelings for him but he has to understand that is about as far as it can go."

The next month, I found out that Karen and Julie were also expecting. Miim is the one that told me, and I could sense the disappointment in his voice.

"Time is running out," he said. "Don't you see if I can't get you pregnant soon, we will miss our chance of having two children. My father asked me just yesterday if we are sleeping together yet. He was very disappointed when I told him that we haven't. He is pushing me hard Angie."

"Is that a good enough reason to make love Miim? Because, your father thinks we should? You told me you wouldn't push me into this Miim and nothing has changed."

"My father is not thinking about making love Angie. He thinks I need to do my part and be more forceful. I'm sorry if that sounds bad to you, but I'm only being honest with you. You know that normally this is not our way of doing things. Morally, it's all wrong, but what choice do we have? It's not like I don't want us to be married. Normally, that is what we do when we want children, but we can't be married when all of our women are already married to others. We feel bad about all this."

"You are saying we. What do you think about it? Miim, you sound like you are being controlled, and your feelings don't make any difference." Now I think he is sensing that I am angry, and briefly he looked away embarrassed. He walked a couple of steps away from me, and put his hands to his head. He stopped, and turned to me. I could tell that he was uncomfortable. He wanted to say something more but I just watched him. He dropped his hands to his sides, and took another few seconds before saying anything.

"Angie, I don't want us to feel these differences. You know how I feel about you and it's more than just a brief relationship." He was hurt and very serious.

"No Miim I don't know how you feel about me. Why don't you tell me?"

"I'm falling in love with you. If I had my way I would want to keep you here with me always, forever Angie, I," he stopped. I guess I didn't realize how shy he really was.

"Have you forgotten that I have children at home?"

"No, and I would never ask you to leave your children. Angie, why don't we have children together and if you decide you don't want me then I will understand." I would rather we come together with love and desire for each other than." He hesitated!

"Than what?"

"Than having to do what the other's, and my father want me to do. It's just not in me to make love to you by force. Angie sometimes I see the way you look at me. I can see it in your eyes. It's like the way I look at you. You have admiration in your eyes, and the way you helped me through grieving. You are so beautiful, and I think you care some about me and you know I'm cute." He said it again with a sweet grin.

"Yes, I think you are very nice. Nicer than I have ever been treated by a man. And yes, cute and the temptation is there sometimes, but that does not make this right. I don't want to fall in love with you. My children are important to me, and one day I would have to make a choice between my children and the children you and I would have together. Miim it hasn't even been three months since I've been here. How can we know our feelings for each other."

"I know how I feel about you. If you were from this planet, I would have chosen you. There would never have been anyone else. Angie, you would not have to make a choice between our children and your children because we could bring your children here to live. They would become mine as well as the ones we have together. Whenever someone here dies, and someone else takes his wife, their children become his. I would love them the same as I would my own. Please understand. What kind of life will your children have now, knowing what you know about John? What kind of life would you have?"

"John is still alive. Do you think he would give up his children? He would fight me for them, Miim. It all sounds good, but he loves his children, and he would never allow me to take them."

"He should have thought of that before sleeping with another woman. You are too good for him to hurt like that, yes? It would serve him right if he lost you and the children. Don't you see, he is the one that broke your wedding vows. His values are not yours. I promise you that I would never do that to you, or your children, if you became mine."

I started to cry. I guess all this was just to much for me to handle right now. He stretched out his arms, and came quickly over to me.

"Come here," he said, but I hesitated.

"Come here," he said again, and I went into his arms. He held me for a minute and let me cry while he stroked my back. It felt good to have an understanding shoulder to cry on. I was ashamed to admit that he felt good. He told me that he was sorry. He did not want me to be upset with him. He then kissed my cheek. I resisted a little, and then he got closer to my lips and I felt myself tighten up. I pulled back but he grabbed me, and drew me close to him.

"Don't pull away from me," he said, almost a little too forceful. He drew me back into his body again and kissed me. At first tenderly, and it felt so wonderful. I couldn't resist. Then, his lips were pressing hard on mine. I could feel the passion in him and his heart beating hard and fast. "I want us to be forever Angie," he whispered. I felt myself responding to him, wanting him. I didn't want to let him go, but I knew this was all wrong.

"No Miim," I felt frightened by his advances, and at the same time my needs were as strong as his. "Let me go," I said trying to push him away from me.

"I'm sorry Angie, but I think you know that we both want each other. Do you think I don't know that you want me as well as I want you? This is gone past making a baby. This is our feelings for each other, yes?" He said this with a little hurt and anger.

"No Miim, we can't do this."

He loosened his hold on me and I broke away from him running to my room. I stayed in there and cried. I made up my mind that I was not going to come out. I needed to think, and sort out my feelings. I was afraid I was giving Miim mixed emotions, and I realized I was falling in love with him too. I just knew things would be worse if I told him. I thought about my children. It would be easy to leave John after what he did to me, but I could never take his children away from him. I can't fall in love with Miim, it would never work. *Oh Miim, what am I doing to you?* I sobbed.

About fifteen minutes later, there came a very faint knock at the door.

"What do you want?" I asked, still sniffling.

"It's me," Miim said in a very soft voice.

I couldn't help but smile to myself. Who does he think I thought it was?

"Can I come in?"

"It's your house."

He opened the door very slowly, "I'm sorry, I had no right do take advantage of you. You're right and unless you're ready, I will not try that again. Can you forgive me?"

"Come over here, sit with me and let's talk. I think your father had a lot to do with what you did. You have been so sweet and great to me. There is nothing to forgive."

"Listen, I just want to be with you, and talk for now. You're right, my father can not push us into something that is not there. We will do whatever we want whenever we want."

"Okay, I'll do it."

"Do what?"

"What you have been wanting me to do, have your baby."

"Do you mean all I had to do was tell you that we're not going to do it, and you would have done it, yes?"

"No, it means I thought about it. I'm mad as hell at John. I've wanted to have another child, he didn't. He cheated on me, I didn't. Why not have your baby? I can decide later what I will do. In the meantime, it is your child and I guess I can give you that. I can't promise I will come back to you. I don't know what will happen, but I do need to go back, and confront John."

"No!" Miim said, as if I'm the one who came up with this idea.

"What do you mean? I thought this is what you want."

"Well yes, no, I mean I don't just want to have a child with you. I want to have a child made out of love. Being mad at John, or pleasing my father should not be the reason to have a child. I meant it when I said that I'm falling in love with you. I will just wait until you feel the same about me. For now you need to get over your feelings for John. I just had a hard time believing you could still love him after cheating on you. I am sorry, I was wrong."

"Miim I do care a lot about you. That's why I decided to give you your child. I just need to be sure about my feelings before I can tell you how I feel."

"I know that you responded to me out there, only if it was just a few seconds. I felt your passion as well as you felt mine, but that's not enough. I think I understand what you are going through. I want us Angie, but I have no one standing in my way like you do. I am confusing you, and I'm sorry."

He said this with a lot of sincerity. He is a wonderful, understanding guy. Why can't it be like this on Earth?

"You're right, I am confused about my feelings. At the same time, I want to please you, and yes, I did respond to you, and at the same time I felt like I had no right to, and I became frightened."

"I'm frightened too, and I understand. Right now I just want to lay down on that bed with you but we will not make love. I just want to hold you, if you will let me, and we will just talk."

I reached up to him and he came into my arms, pulling me close to him. He stroked my hair, and kissed my cheek, and told me that he is crazy about me. "I will be here when you are really ready," he whispered.

He felt so good next to my body and I wanted more, but we both knew it wasn't the time. And so, we talked until wee hours in the morning holding each other affectionately.

The next day, I had lunch with Ann, Krista and Tammie. They talked about their being pregnant. They seemed so happy about it, and they were crazy about their guys. They talked about names for their babies, and how each got treated. They all made a decision to stay if they can get their children. They never felt as happy as they are now. I could almost feel the twinge of jealousy, as I thought about how good Miim felt next to me and how sweet he has been.

"What about you Angie? You have to have some feelings for Miim," Tammie asked.

"Yes, I do but he is giving me more time, we're just not ready yet. He is very understanding and caring." In my heart I knew I was feeling more and when we get home from dinner I think it's about time I showed him. I'm starting to miss him whenever he is gone, and I just can't wait to see him. I guess I am falling for him. I have never in my life felt this good about a man before. I think last night, I learned what true love is all about.

"Well that's a start," Tammie said, very excited for me. "I was hoping you would make a decision to stay here."

"I haven't decided that far in advance. I only know how Miim makes me feel."

That night when we went to dinner, Miim stayed, mostly, very close to me. When he did get up to get something, I couldn't take my eyes off him. He stopped to talk to Sem Diao Miim for just a minute and a couple times he glanced my way, and each time caught me looking at him. I wondered what they were saying, but mostly I felt shy about flirting with him and he knew I was doing just that. I smiled at him when he came back. He touched my arm and ran his fingers across my cheek in such a loving way, and I felt that he was feeling this magic that I was feeling. I wondered again if he could read my mind.

"Derrif and Ann are going to have a baby," he smiled.

"Miim, I"

"Shhhhh don't say a word, it's okay. Did I tell you that you look beautiful tonight?"

"I'm not beautiful," and I really believed that, but he is so sweet to keep telling me.

"Yes you are, and I'm crazy about you," he said smiling. "Let's go home early, I just want to be alone with you. I enjoyed our time together last night."

The thing is, he really made me feel beautiful and special. I could sense his love. I loved the way he was looking me, and I believe he was thinking the same thing. On the way home I would glance up at him again, and he would catch me and smile down at me. He put his arm around me and pulled me closer to him.

"I know what you're thinking and it won't work," he said, as he looked down at me and winked.

"What am I thinking?"

"You're thinking that you didn't want to be the last one to have a baby."

"Oh, so you guys do read minds, do you?"

"Kind of!"

"Well your way off," or was he?

When we got in the door I told him I wanted to change into something more comfortable.

"Can I come in after awhile? I want to stay with you. Don't worry, I will not go back on my word. There is something I want to tell you."

"Sure, there is something I want to tell you too. Give me five minutes before you come in."

When Miim came in, he did not see me. "knock knock," he said out loud.

"I'm in your bath, come in."

When he came in he looked at me, he knew, there was wanting in his eyes and also in mine. There were candles all around and soft music playing.

"Are you sure?" he asked.

"I'm sure!"

He started unbuttoning his shirt, and allowed it to fall where he was. He sat down on a bench to take off his shoes. He watched me, as I was splashing water over myself, and he smiled. I smiled back at him. He took off all of his clothes, and threw them on the floor. I watched him as he slowly walked down the steps, into the warm water, totally naked. He watched me, as I was watching him, neither of us feeling embarrassed. He reached over to turn on a suds machine that splashed and made bubbles. I could not take my eyes off of him, and I never in my life wanted anyone more. He looked so wonderful. He reached for me, and I moved swiftly in his arms.

"Are you sure, no?" he asked again, as he touched my face.

"I am sure, yes, I thought you guys could read minds."

He took me in his arms and kissed me. I wanted him and he knew it. He pulled me closer to him and we made love for the first time. I had never in my life experienced anything like it. He was so tender, sweet, loving. and so good, so patient.

"I love you," he said when we were trying to calm down. "You are my first and only."

"I love you too Miim," I said.

"You do? Do you mean it?"

"Of course I do."

"Angie," he said with tears in his eyes, "does that mean that you will stay with me."

"I don't know Miim. Give me time. I don't even want to think about it right now. Let's just enjoy each other for now."

That night we held each other all night, sometimes talking, sometimes sleeping, but this time we were under the covers, naked, feeling the excitement from each others body. We made love again.

He told me again and again how much he wanted me and loved me and I told him how much I loved him.

"Hey, what were you and your dad talking about?" I asked him later, as I was brushing the hair from his forehead with my fingers.

"He asked me if we slept together yet, and I told him no, but tonight was the night."

"Oh your terrible," I said, as he was laughing.

"Miim, you never told me what you wanted to talk to me about, you know, you said earlier that you wanted to talk to me about something."

"Well now, maybe I just made that up so I could stay with you tonight."

"Did you?"

"Did I what?"

"Did you make it up so you could sleep with me?"

"No, the truth is, I knew that we were going to make love tonight. I felt the connection. Don't be mad at me, but I wanted to explain some things about me before we made love. I wanted you to know that I had never been with anyone before and I wanted to make it right. I wasn't sure if I knew how."

"Miim, you were wonderful, don't change anything. I have loved you for awhile but now I love you even more."

"Angie I love you too," he said, and I could feel his tears on my face. "What did you want to talk to me about."

"What are you talking about?"

"Come on, when I told you I wanted to talk to you, you said you wanted to talk to me too, yes."

"I wanted to let you know that I was ready to make love with you. I will deal with things later, but tonight it's just you and me."

"Do you think we made a baby tonight?"

"Yes, I think we did."

The next couple of months were about the same. I did some chores around the house, and I started writing down things, so I would later remember them. It gave me something to do. I was feeling more comfortable about taking long walks, and I would shop and sometimes have a few friends over. Mostly, I couldn't wait for Miim to come home. He didn't want me to do any hard work in case I got pregnant, and he wanted to be sure we didn't lose it. One day, he came home and found me crying, and laying down on the bed.

"Angie what's wrong?" he came running over to me.

"I'm sorry, I'm so sorry," I sobbed.

"Sweetheart, tell me what has you so upset."

"I'm not pregnant," I said still sobbing as I went into his arms. "I'm sorry!"

"Oh baby, don't worry, that doesn't mean it won't happen. It just means we might have to wait a little longer."

"But we have been making love for two months now. I should have gotten pregnant, and I'm afraid we will run out of time."

"No, even if we only have one child, we still have plenty of time. I tell you what, let's go out to eat. You go freshen up. We will try to find the Doctor and see what he can tell us. If we don't get pregnant it isn't your fault. We both have been trying very hard."

He made me smile, he just had a way to make me feel better, and good about myself. God, I love this man so much.

The Doctor told us it could be stress, or maybe just trying too hard. He told us to try to wait a few days and if I couldn't get pregnant within the next two months, he would run some tests. On the way home, Miim teased me about, he didn't know how we can stop trying so hard, but he would give it a try. Our instructions were to make love no more than three days a week and put time between. We still stayed together at night, but it was difficult to keep away from each other when we both had so much desire.

The Doctor was right, about two months later I found out that I was pregnant. After doing the test I couldn't wait for Miim to get home to tell him. Maybe I shouldn't have told him yet, because after the excitement was over, he pampered me and showered me with love and attention. When we went to the dining hall Miim made the announcement that we were expecting a baby. Since I was the last one to get pregnant, everyone clapped and cheered. Miim was so happy. His father was the first to congratulate us. He came over to me and told me that he was very proud of me.

"You remind me of my wife, and I know that you will be a great mother." I hugged him and thanked him. I told him I was honored, and he was going to be a wonderful grandfather. As we were walking back to our table, we thought it was amusing to see so many pregnant women at the same time.

Everything was going great for the next couple of months, except for some morning sickness. I was very happy, although, I was missing my children. Miim would help me through that by telling me he couldn't wait to bring them here. I would have to remind him that it may not happen. The next couple of months, my pregnancy became difficult. I passed out several times and Miim did not want to leave me. He had people check up on me several times a day, and he called me every hour. He came home at lunch time to check up on me, and he would always bring me something to eat.

I was between my fifth and sixth month when I started to get awful cramps and started to bleed. I called Miim to come home, but he sent for the medics to get me and he met me at the hospital. He was so worried and he told me that we would never have another child. He was blaming himself. I stayed at the hospital for several days and Miim took leave to stay with me, after I was well enough to go home. I had to stay down and walk no more than 100 steps a day. Miim was so funny because he would not let me get up without him, and he counted every step. Most of the time he picked me up and carried me.

One day, after being on Cribaar almost a year, Miim came home with a very sad look on his face and tears in his eyes. I knew him well enough to know that something dreadful was wrong.

"Ann and Derrif lost their baby last night," he said, now with tears streaming down his eyes.

"Oh no, oh no," I found myself saying as I went into his arms. "What happened Miim?"

"We don't know yet. Ann has been very healthy. We can't figure it out. Angie whatever you do, please take care of yourself. We almost lost our baby once. I couldn't stand it if anything happened to you, or our baby."

"I'm fine Miim, what did she have?" I guessed her to be about eight months pregnant.

"A boy," he said, drawing me closer to him. "I need to go, Honey."

"I want to go with you."

"No, I don't want you to get stressed out, this could happen to us. I didn't even want to tell you, but I knew you would hear it from someone else. Please, you stay here, yes. I will bring you something to eat."

I knew he was right. My pregnancy has been pretty shaky, not to mention how long it took for me to conceive.

Miim came home again, he didn't say much and I could tell that he was upset.

"How are Ann and Deriff holding up?" I asked.

"They're taking it pretty hard, but they will be okay."

"Do you know what happened?"

"Not yet, but the Doctor was there. He wants to check her out further and he won't let her get pregnant again until they can figure it out. She was bleeding a lot, and we were very worried, but the Doctor was able to get it under control. She wants you to come over tomorrow. Honey, please don't stay long or get stressed out."

"Miim, I will be okay, I promise."

The next day, I visited Ann. Miim insisted on taking me, and he told me he would pick me up in about an hour. Derrif knew that I was coming, and he needed to go out to do chores while I stayed with her.

"Are you okay?" I asked him, as he was on his way out.

"I'm okay, it was tough on her, see what you can do."

"Okay, I will stay with her until you get back."

"Thanks Angie, you and Miim have been great. Ann thinks a lot of you," he said as I walked toward her room.

"Ann," I ran over to her and put my hand on her cheek. "Oh Ann."

"Don't worry, I'll be okay. I'm just worried about him, he really wanted this child."

"I know he did Ann. What can I do?"

"Just being here helps Angie, thanks. We appreciate Miim being here last night. You guys are great friends."

"Thanks Ann, you guys are great too. Do you know what caused the problem?"

"Not yet, it could be stress related. I overheard the men talking and they are blaming themselves for pushing us so hard, and wanting us to start having babies as soon as we got here. Miim has been so worried something like this will happen to you. You can look forward to being pampered for the next few months."

"I'm already pampered. I wouldn't know what else he could do. I wanted to come last night but he was afraid that I would get stressed out."

"I know and he is right. Angie, how are you and the baby?"

"I'm doing a lot better after the scare. The Doctors think I will be fine and Miim started back to work last week. Don't worry about me Ann, just get yourself well. I will be here for you, and if you need to talk, call me."

"Thanks Angie"

The next few months went well. Babies were being delivered one right after the other. Tammie had the first one, a girl, they named Rachay. Several boys were born the next couple of weeks and just as we thought there were not going to be any more girls, six couples in a row had girls. Two were born on the same day almost within the hour. Each day that a baby was born, Miim came home so excited. He watched over me and cared for me and of course I took it all in and loved every minute of it.

A couple weeks later, we found out that we were going to have a girl. If you think Miim was happy before, you should have seen him then. When we went out that night he couldn't wait to tell his father. I could hear them both from across the room and they were hugging each other. Sem Diao Miim came over to tell me that I made them both very happy. He also asked if he could be a part of the baby's life.

"Of course, you are already a part of the baby's life. You are going to be her grandpa."

"I'm going to spoil her like crazy, and I will teach her so many things and."

"Wait," I said, "let's wait until she is born and we'll take one thing at a time."

"I'm just so excited Angle. I just wish Karis could be here for her grandchild. She would have loved you."

"Thanks, that is a compliment."

That evening Miim told me that he wanted me to name her.

"I want to be able to call her something other than it," he said smiling.

"I can name her anything I want?"

"Sure, whatever it is, I know I will love it."

"Well that is very good because, I have a name already picked out."

"Great, what is it? and please, don't make it to awful."

"But you said you will love it no matter what I pick out."

"Okay, your keeping me in suspense, what is it?"

"I thought we would name her Dani, after your sister."

He stared at me in disbelief and a look of sadness came over him. He just stood staring at me, and I thought I made a big mistake and I said, "well we can name her something else if you think that would be too upsetting."

"No, I love it, do you know how much I love you for even thinking of it?"

"I think I can guess." You had me worried for a minute. I thought I made a big mistake."

"You are wonderful." He grabbed me up in his arms, and told me again that he loved me. "Dani it is and I can't wait until my father hears this. He's going to love it. He loves you too Angie, you know that, yes?"

CHAPTER SIX

"Carrie, I fell hard for this man. I just don't know what to do."

"What does your heart tell you?"

"Of course I want to be with him, but I have to think of the kids. Gosh, I am not even divorced. I'm carrying around all this guilt."

About that time the phone rang and Carrie got up to answer it. "Yes, she's here. No, but she is upset. Give her some time John, she needs to think things through. Yes she did, you knew she would. I don't know, she didn't say. Okay, I will tell her, okay."

"What does he want?"

"I think he's checking up on you. He wanted to know if you told me about the years you were missing. He also wants to know if you plan to be home tonight. Are you?"

"I guess I had better talk to him. I just don't want him to touch me."

"Be careful Angie. I don't know if you should trust him. If he tries anything, you call me. I will come get you."

"I'll be okay. I won't take his threats seriously."

"Angie, I would miss you terribly if you left, but you need to be with Miim. I have never seen you so happy, confused yes, but happy. I know that you love this man, and John does not deserve you. Don't feel bad about leaving him. I am your friend and I would not tell you this unless I meant it. Get away from John."

"Thanks Carrie, I guess I needed to hear that."

That night, when I went home, I decided to get some of my things together. I wanted to do it before he got home just in case he did try anything. Maybe he will get the idea we need some time apart. When he came in he said he wanted to take me out to dinner. Although, I was not up to it, I decided to go in case he was in a bad mood. He wouldn't try anything while other people were around. I told him I needed to go get ready and he followed me up to the spare bedroom where I was staying. He was reminding me of all the good things that we did together and how much fun we had when we were dating. I couldn't help to think about Miim and the fun we had. There was no comparison.

"What is this? Where are you going?" he said with a loud voice when he saw my suitcases.

"I don't know yet. It depends how things are going between us, and if I feel that I have to leave. I'm sorry but your threat made me mistrust you."

"You're making me out to be some kind of monster, Angie. I've never once beat you or anything."

"You've shoved me up against the door and screamed at me," I reminded him. "You have grabbed my arm and put bruises on me on many occasions. Not to mention you threatened my life yesterday. Look John let's just go out and talk and see how it goes." In actuality, I felt a little frightened of him, but I didn't want him to know.

"You know that I would never really hurt you, Angie."

"Do I?"

John took me to our favorite restaurant. I guess he considered this as a date for a new beginning. As soon as we got seated he asked me to forgive him. He said he wanted to start over, if I would just take him back. He reached for my hand but I drew back.

"I have to give this a lot of thought John, this much hurt does not just go away."

"I told you Angie, Kay does not mean anything to me, it's you I love."

"But I am in love with another man John, I told you that. I had no intentions of that happening until I found out that you had an affair. I wanted to have his baby. I didn't think that I could ever love you again when I found out what you did so I just decided to make a new life for myself. I want to go back to him John. I can't forgive you."

"I thought you told me everything Angie." I sensed anger in his voice.

"I did tell you John, but you didn't take me seriously. Even before I was gone, I wondered if our marriage was going to last. You and I both know that we were having some problems." The whole time I was talking, he was looking at me with disbelief and disgust, like how could I do this to him.

"Do you mean to tell me that you were screwing around with another man at your own free will and you led me to believe that your were raped?"

"Well I guess if you want to put it that way, but keep in mind I never would have gone along with their plan if you hadn't screwed around, as you put it." He now sensed the anger in my voice and was not at all used to my talking back to him.

"You bitch, at least I didn't fall in love with Kay."

I got up to leave before we had a chance to order. I was not going to stay around and take mental abuse from him, but not before I said to him, "so that makes it okay."

"Where are you going?" He shouted as he got up to chase after me. He was a few steps behind me, because he had to throw money down to pay for our drinks. He caught up with me outside. He grabbed a hold of my arm and twisted it around my back, and I cried out in pain.

"You bitch," he said again. "You know I will never let you leave me again. If you do, you will never see your children again, ever. Do you understand me?"

"You're hurting me John, what are you going to do, hold me a prisoner?"

"Let her go," a mans voice behind us said. He was loud, demanding.

"Mind your own business, she's my wife and I will handle her as I please." John let me go and I turned around and there stood Miim. *Oh my God, Miim, no, please no.*

"It's okay Mister," I said to him with pleading eyes. "Were just having a bit of a disagreement, but everything is fine." I could feel my heart racing. I could not believe he is here watching over me. That's all I need for John to find out who he is. Miim looked at me for a few seconds longer, and turned to walk away. *Oh Lord help me,* I thought.

John took my elbow gently, and guided me to the car.

"Let's talk about this tomorrow John. Right now I'm still confused with my feelings and I need time to think."

"You know that you will not divorce me." He said it as a threat.

He did not say anything else on the way home and as soon as we got there I went on up to the guest room. Before leaving Miim the last time, he had given me a key ring with a small disc on a key. If I needed to get in touch with him, all I needed to do was squeeze the disc and wait outside of the shopping center, and he would be there within a few minutes. Tomorrow, after John leaves for work, I thought I would do just that. I needed to see Miim to warn him to stay away. I couldn't stand the thought of him getting caught or hurt.

I entered the kitchen the next morning. John was sitting and reading the paper. "Coffee's over there," he said.

"Thanks, John, I promise I will make a decision tonight, that is unless you've already decided that I am a bitch."

"Don't be stupid Angie, you know that I called you that because you had me upset."

I could only think, *he sure has a weird way of trying hard to make this marriage work.*

"Are you going out?" He asked, glancing up at me and then down at his paper.

"I will probably go over to Carrie's after I do a little shopping."

"I meant what I said last night, if you leave, you will never see the kids again."

As soon as John left, I called Carrie. "I need to talk to you. There is something I need to do first but I can be over there this afternoon."

"Yes, and I need to hear the rest of this story."

"Do you want me to bring Miim?"

"Of course, but aren't you afraid of getting caught?"

"I doubt that will happen, but if it does, I will have to confront the two. I told John last night that I love Miim and he has threatened me with the children. I will tell you all about it when I get there."

"Come on over for lunch."

"Thanks Carrie, I love you," I smiled.

After talking to Carrie, I went on up to shower, straighten my room and headed on out. I was getting excited about seeing Miim and Dani. They were staying in a space craft a few miles from town. They would move it around to keep from being discovered and they also kept it covered. I myself, did not know where it was. It had several smaller bedrooms in it that Miim and I shared with Dani. On the way back to Earth, Miim was quiet, and I knew he was upset about my seeing John. I think he was afraid that I wouldn't be able to get away from him. He told me that he would come for me whenever I pushed the button on the small disc.

I took a taxi to the shopping center and when I got close I took out the key ring and squeezed the disc. I got there a few minutes later and within another few minutes there was Miim. I ran to him making sure that no one was around. He took me in his arms and kissed me but it was brief because of the fear of getting caught.

"I miss you terribly," he said, looking at me. Both of us wanted to be together. "Let's go back to the ship for the rest of the day. It will give us a chance to talk and among other things. Did John hurt you?"

"I'm fine, he just has to show me who is boss every now and then."

"I can't stand him touching you. I wanted to kill him for hurting you."

"I know, but please, you have to stay away. I want you to come with me to Carrie's. I told her most of our story, up until I was pregnant. I promised I would tell her the rest this afternoon. Come on she is going to have lunch for us."

"Are you sure you want to take that chance?"

"Well you took a big one last night."

"I'm not going to stand by and allow him to abuse you, Angie."

"I don't think he would really hurt me. Come on, I'll take you with me and give us a chance to talk in the taxi."

When we got in the taxi Miim said, "I want you to leave him now Angie, please. I'm so worried about you. I think he treats you badly and it will only get worse."

Miim, you have got to stop following me around and watching over me. I will be alright, but that scared the hell out of me last night. He can't know who you are. You told me I have two months before the ship goes back. You know I need that time. I still don't have the kids. He told me if I leave, I would never see my children again. I still haven't made up my mind about going back."

"I think you have. We love each other."

"I know, but that doesn't make everything right and you have to promise me you will not keep watching out for me. I have to do things my way, without you. Promise me Miim. You know that we could get caught if you are always around. I was afraid that he was going to start a fight with you."

"You told him that you love me, yes?

"Yes, that's why he hurt me. Miim if I leave now, I may never see the kids again. He could easily get them and hide them from me. My parents are taking his side on this."

"I can't let him hurt you again, but I understand that you have to do this your way. I don't want you to lose the children."

"Give me three weeks, just three weeks, that's when the kids get out of school and I will let you know something, okay?"

He agreed but reluctantly.

"Tell me about Dani, I can't wait to see her."

"She's been a little cranky. I think she is missing her mother."

We arrived at Carrie's, and although she knew Miim may be coming, she seemed a little surprised. After introducing him to her, she told us to come in. We went to sit on the patio near the pool. Miim told her he loved her place.

Carrie went to get drinks and when she got back, she told me that John had called or was she not suppose to say anything in front of Miim.

"I tell him everything. What did John want? Checking to make sure I'm not skipping out on him, I suppose."

"I told him that you were on your way over and you would be here for lunch. I tell you true Angie, I never did think John was good enough for you. Grant thinks the same thing. He never did like him. John seems to think that I can talk to you and let you know what could happen if you left him. He wanted me to tell you what you would be missing. To tell you the truth Angie, it sounded to me like a threat."

"I'm trying to convince her to come stay with me, Miim said, looking very worried. I can go get your children and we could hide out until we leave.

"Carrie, I'm trying to tell Miim that it wouldn't be that easy. He could be arrested for kidnapping the kids. It would only frighten them."

"I'm willing to take that chance, just to have all of you with me. Who is Grant?"

"Grant is a friend and a cop. I think I told you about him, Sgt. Wayne." I told Miim, as he looked at me curiously."

"Now, before we have lunch I want to hear about your little girl. What happened next?" Carrie asked.

Miim couldn't help to start the conversation out to tell Carrie about Dani. He started with how she got her name and how beautiful she is. "She is a little over a year old now and she looks like her beautiful mommy. She has my dark curly hair." Miim showed her the picture he carried, and then the one he took of us after she was born.

"And your smile," I reminded him.

"I agree, she is beautiful, like her mommy. So, you never had another child?" Carrie asked.

"No Angie had a hard time getting pregnant and when she finally did she almost lost her. She also had a tough delivery. We decided not to have another child."

"You decided, I didn't."

"I do not want to put her through that again," Miim told Carrie."

"But I am fine now and we will decide later."

Miim smiled and I knew he was thinking that I planned to go back with him.

"Excuse him Carrie, he has this idea that I'm going back with him."

"Come on Angie," Carrie said, "help me bring out our lunch, and then we can talk some more."

"Okay but be careful what you say to me, I think Miim reads minds." Miim smiled as we walked in the kitchen.

"Can I help?" he asked.

"No, this will give us a chance to talk about you," Carrie teased. "Wow, he is so handsome, he looks like a movie star and that neat accent. Angie, you are so lucky, and the pictures of your little girl. Oh Angie, how can you give all that up?"

"That's the problem, I don't know if I can. I just have to think about it Carrie. I need more time than he is giving me, but I have to put my children first. I can't just go pick them up and leave. If I decide to go back with him I have to wait until the spaceship is about ready to go back. If John catches me, there is no telling what he would do. If I don't go, at least I know that Miim is a wonderful father and Dani will be taken care of."

"I can't believe all of this. You have to realize Angie, all of what's been happening with you was hard to believe, but I am understanding more now. I think you have made up your mind to go back with him. I will do any thing to help you. We will come up with a plan."

"Yes I think I knew all along that I would go back with him, but if Miim knows that he will want me to go now. I have to protect him and the others that are here. Even Grant has made threats. I will tell you about that next time we get together."

After lunch was over, we talked awhile. I told Miim I wanted to get home before John did. On the way back he seemed quiet except for saying that he liked Carrie, and was glad that I had her as a friend.

"I feel better that she will be coming over to your house to check on you once in a while since you won't let me do it. I don't like you there, Angie."

Again, I reassured him that I would be okay.

"Miim please be careful, Grant knows you are here and he has made threats."

"I know, Tammie has already warned us. Honey we will be fine, except I'm worried about you."

"You do whatever you have to do to protect our daughter, even if you have to leave without me. Please say you will leave without me if it means protecting our daughter Miim. You do agree don't you?"

He looked at me, fretting but he did not say a word.

After getting back we had just about two hours. Long enough for him to take me to see Dani. She was just waking up from a nap but we managed to play with her a bit. When I asked Miim to take me back to the shopping center, he grabbed me up and kissed me, and said, "something is going to go wrong, I can feel it." I held him tightly and wished I had more time with him. I needed him and I could sense that he needed me. As I said good by to the others I could feel a loss. I thought it was strange that Miim said he felt something was going to go wrong. Carrie had said the same thing. I told him that and I added, "Nothing is going to go wrong, don't think that."

"Please be careful, I love you."

"I love you too."

As we approached the shopping center, he asked when he could see me again.

"I will keep in contact." My heart was breaking and I knew his was too. "We are taking too big of a risk and we have to protect our daughter." I felt a need to say it again. I had to know he would go without me if he needed to go.

"I know!"

On the way home I picked up Chinese food and got there about a half hour before John did. I had time to tidy up the house a bit but I decided John can do his own room. I used to clean up after him. Now that I thought about it, he expected me to do it.

When John came in, he threw his briefcase on the sofa. He told me he was not ready for dinner yet. He came over to me and asked me if I made a decision.

"Yes, I know what I'm going to do." I looked at him long and hard. I guess he felt that something was wrong, or it might have been the look on my face. He didn't wait for my answer. Before I knew it, he pushed me up against the wall, and had a hold of my hair, pulling it until I cried in pain.

"You will not leave here, you understand. No other man will touch you again. It's been three years since we've done this and I want you right now."

"No John, stop it." I cried, as he forced himself against me putting his mouth against mine.

"You're my wife Angie, and it's about time you're acting like it." He started to unbutton my blouse and I could feel his hardness next to me still pushing me up against the wall. He smelled like he had been drinking beer, a stale familiar smell. I believe he had it all planned out what he would do if I decided to leave him.

"Do you think I'm going to let some alien screw my wife and I can't?"

He was tearing at my clothes. I was no match for him and although I tried to fight him off, I knew that I would have to endure what he was about to do to me. When the phone rang. he looked at me, and gave me a push and walked over to the phone.

"What is it?" I heard him ask in a harsh tone. "hello, hello!"

At the same time, I prayed whoever was on that phone would hear me cry out.

"Leave me alone," I screamed. I just had enough time to bolt out of the kitchen, run up to my room and lock it.

He was following me up the stairs when he said. "Angie, Angie, I'm sorry. I would never really take advantage of you, you know that."

He was outside the bedroom door pleading for me to come out so we can talk, but I was still shaken and I told him that I didn't trust him. At first he started beating on the door but after about fifteen minutes he went away. I was wishing there was a phone in my room. I couldn't believe it, he was going to rape me. My God, what do I do? I wanted to call Carrie, I wanted to call Grant. I waited, afraid that he was going to burst down the door. I couldn't hear anything, and this made me even more afraid. I wished now that I would have gone on up to get the kids but, I knew my parents would have warned him and he would have caught me before I could get away. What did Miim know when he said something is going to go wrong? How could he have known? Carrie said it too. Am I the only fool around here? I've got to have a plan to get the kids. In the meantime, I have already sent for my new license. I just have to wait until they come. I will tell John that I plan to visit the kids for awhile and when school is out, I will take the kids away, and even my parents won't know. I will get out of town fast, and I will call Miim to come get me. I can tell the kids as we are driving away, and that way they won't let out our little secret. What will I tell the kids about their father? I have to think, school will be out soon and I don't have everything thought out. Oh Lord, help me carry out this plan, I prayed. I'm shaking hard and I'm not thinking correctly. I hadn't even thought about eating. I just stayed in my room. I did not want to be near John again. All I could think of is how to get the kids and be with Miim.

I could not hear John again, so, after planning an escape, I went on to bed. I couldn't sleep, I was frightened of what John might do. I will leave him tomorrow. I will get a hold of Miim again and tell him that I'm going to go on up to stay with my parents until school is out, and then make a run for it. I will give him a day that we can meet and I will stay with him until the spacecraft is ready to go. It would have been easier if we came back to Earth when the kids were out of school, but we needed to get back for other men to pick up other women. Some of the women that were already on Cribaar had a second child and we waited until the last child was born before we could make the journey back. There was only a few women that was planned to go to Cribaar for the first time. Most of the ones that were already there wanted to go back there, but came here for their children.

I tried to keep my mind on Miim and how he made me feel, so gentle. John never knew how to treat a woman, but I didn't realize it until I made love with Miim. He took his time with me and I felt his passion, where John was quick and only thought about himself. I was laying there with all these things going through my head and I sat up with a start. I smelled smoke or was I dozing off, thinking about Miim and just imagined it. *No, it is smoke*, I thought as I jumped out of bed. My God, he is trying to kill me. He set a fire to the house. He wants me dead so he can get the insurance money and the kids. I remembered his threats, and his voice was going through my head. He threatened me and told me, I would never see the children again if I left. Help me God, he wants to make sure I don't get the kids.

I ran to the door and screamed. "John, help me, John!" The smoke was getting thicker but I did not hear John, and the door was locked on the outside. I screamed again and again, but no one heard my cries. I turned on the light and looked around the room, my purse had the disc in it. I left my purse down stairs, damn, how could I be so careless. There was no lock on the outside of this door, then why can't I open it? Damn him, somehow he locked me in here. I ran to a window. I needed to get some air, it was locked. I tried to unlock it, but it was jammed. *That bastard is trying to kill me. He had this planned all along.* I picked up a chair to throw against the window. The smoke was getting heavier. I tried to scream again, but I started coughing, and no scream would come out. Smoke was filling my lungs, and I had to act and act quick.

Miim help me, if you can hear me, please help me. I threw the chair, but the window did not break. I picked it up and threw it again. This time the window shattered into small fragments. I could get some air, but I had to get out. Although, I did not see flames, the smoke was getting thicker and my lungs were hurting. There was no one here to help me. I looked down to the patio. It looked so far down, and there was nothing to climb down on. I ran to the other window, but figured if I jump out of this one, I would land on the patio furniture. I kept coughing from the smoke and I couldn't breath. I felt myself passing out, and my knees were dropping to the floor. I knew I was slipping away. I decided I had to jump now, or die. That's when I forced myself up with what energy I had left. I sat on the window sill to try to get air but the smoke was getting worse. I turned around and I went out the broken window, remembering what Carrie and Miim said about something is going to go wrong. I then lowered myself as low as I could go, and prayed as I let go.

CHAPTER SEVEN

It's so dark in here. I have to find my way out. I called to Miim. Why can't he hear me? I can see him at the end of the tunnel. I know it's him, but yet he is not responding to me. I woke up, but no one was there so I came back here. It feels safe here and I keep hearing Miim's voice but he can't hear me. There is a handle on the wall, it looks like a handle used for handicapped people. I went to it and tried to grab it thinking it would help me get up. Get up? I didn't even know that I was lying on the floor. How did I get here? I tried to reach the handle, but my hand would not move. I tried to sit up but my body became heavy. I heard voices, that's it! I'm back on the space ship. It's Miim's voice I hear. I tried to call to him but nothing would come out. I tried screaming to him. My mouth was open but I couldn't hear myself scream. Why is it so dark in here? I felt tears rolling down my cheeks. I didn't want Miim to see me cry. He would find out that I got hurt. I got hurt? I don't remember getting hurt, but yet my head was hurting. Now I can feel pain all over my body. Why is everyone leaving me here when I am in so much pain? I think I just have a headache. The end of the tunnel is coming now, it's coming very fast. Miim isn't at the end anymore. There is other voices but I can't make out what they are saying. I can hear them more clearly now. They are closer. They are telling me that I need to come back now or I may never have another chance. They are shouting at me. I don't know where I'm suppose to go. I don't want to go back there because I might get hurt again. Something is going to hurt me. Miim, help me, the voices are coming. I know they are bad. They are trying to hurt me again. Why can't he hear me anymore? I can feel someone touch me but it wasn't a person. It was something dangerous. I tried to run, I had to get away but the thing was faster than I was. It jumped on me and I am screaming. I can scream now. I don't have to worry anymore. I can scream.

CHAPTER EIGHT

"Miim, can you hear me?"

"I can hear you. I'm right here."

"I can't see you."

"I'm right here. I'm touching your hand."

"I can feel it. You shouldn't be here. You might get caught. You need to go now, I will catch up to you."

"I can't leave you. You're hurt, I have to be with you."

When I woke up, John was sitting in a chair next to my bed. "John what happened, where am I?"

John quickly jumped up and leaned over me. "You're awake, you're in the hospital Honey"

"What happened John?" I said weakly. I noticed my voice was gruff. I didn't sound like myself at all.

"You're in the hospital Honey" he said again. "You've been here for several weeks now. How are you feeling? I've been so worried."

"No, I've got to go, I'm running late." I tried to lift my head, but I couldn't lift it. It felt so heavy and I was getting so dizzy. "What happened to me John?" I could feel my tears running down my face. Why did John look like he had smoke all around his face?

"Lie still, you have been hurt, but you will be okay now. There was a fire in the house Honey. I'm sorry we lost some of our stuff. The house was in bad shape but repairs are being done now. Everything is going to be okay. Angie I have been so worried about you." he repeated. "I'll be right back. I want to go tell the nurse that you're awake."

"Wait, where are the kids? We were suppose to get them."

Why is he acting like nothing is wrong? Doesn't he believe I'm leaving him? He is treating me like nothing ever happened. He is the one that did this to me. I've got to get out of here. I've got to find Miim. He will leave without me. Oh no, he doesn't know that I am here and he thinks that I wanted to stay with John.

"The Doctor will be here in a while," he said as he came back through the door. John smiled at me and said. "I'm so glad you're back. I couldn't stand it if anything happened to you."

"John, the kids, where are they?"

"Don't worry about them. Your parents are taking good care of them. They have been here to see you and they know they will not be able to come home yet."

"John, it's not fair. We promised them we would get them."

"It's going to be a long time before you are well enough to take the kids Honey. I'm sorry, but you had a nasty fall, and you've been in a coma."

Miim, where are you? I need you.

"I've been in a coma? How long will I be here?" Already I was planning an escape, I had to find Miim, I had to talk to Carrie.

"Almost six weeks. I'm so glad you remember me," John said, sounding to chipper. "The Doctors told me that there might be brain damage and you might not ever remember things. You had a pretty tough go of it Angie. Do you remember anything at all?"

About that time the Doctor came in, "Hello sleepy head," he teased. "We were beginning to wonder if you were ever going to get out of that bed." He checked me out and turned to John. "Don't stay too much longer. Her blood pressure is up and she will need complete rest. I will schedule her for some tests tomorrow and if all goes well you may be able to take her home before the week is out."

No, I was screaming inside. *Don't they know that he is the reason I'm in here? He should be in jail. I can't go home with him. He will try to kill me again.*

"How long have I been here Doctor? What happened to me?"

"Do you remember anything of what happened?" he asked.

"There was a fire and I jumped out the window. How did I get here?"

"Your husband called the ambulance. You hit your head and you had a few stitches, but if you take it easy it looks like you will be fine. Our main concern was whether you would gain your memory back or not. It looks like you do remember some things. It's a good sign. It will probably be a lot longer before most of your memory comes back, or you may never recall everything."

After he left I looked over to see if I could reach the phone. I noticed there was none. "Would you call Carrie for me John? I want to see her."

"Now Honey, you heard what the Doctor said, you need rest to get well. We'll talk about it tomorrow." John turned around toward the Doctor at the door and I saw John motion to him. They went on out in the hall and they were talking. I could not hear everything they said no matter how hard I tried. The only thing I heard was John saying absolutely no visitors.

John came back in the room. He told me he would check on me tomorrow. He will tell me everything then, but for now, I needed to get some rest. When he left he closed the door and I felt very lonely. I was trying to think, but everything was so confusing. I could only think about Miim, and leaving John. *Why is John acting like nothing is wrong between us?* Later, when a nurse came in, I asked her to call the police and ask for Grant Wayne. I also ask her not to tell my husband because he wants me dead. "Please, I need help."

"Okay Sweetie," she said, with a lot of sincerity. "I'll see if he is available. Now you stop worrying. You are in good hands and nothing is going to happen to you. Your husband seems like a nice guy. He has been here several hours a day and he was worried about you." She appeared to be calming me down, as she was checking some tubes coming from all the equipment that was in my room.

"No, he is not, he is only pretending to be worried. He is the reason I'm here. Please get me some help." *Why doesn't she believe me?*

"Okay Sweetie, you get some rest and I will see what I can do." She then gave me a shot of something and I did not wake up until the next morning.

The Doctor came in again shortly after breakfast. "Good morning," he said a little bit too friendly to a person that is about to be killed by her husband. "I see they have you sitting up a little bit. How are you feeling?"

"Scared, didn't the nurse tell you that my husband is trying to kill me? I need help!"

"Now, now" he said very calmly, "We're not going to let anyone kill you. You will be fine. We're going to take very good care of you. I will ask the nurse to give you something to help you relax. See if you can eat a little more of that breakfast. It will help you get well and out of here faster."

"I don't want to sleep anymore. I want to stay awake so I can think."

He came over to me and did that thing with the light in the eyes. He started to feel all over my head. *This guy thinks I'm crazy. What did John tell them? They don't believe me.* I could feel myself panic. "I need you to call the police for me, please," I pleaded. *Can't he hear the fear in my voice?*

"Okay, don't get excited, this won't help you get well. Your blood pressure is high, and you have to calm down."

"The reason my blood pressure is up is because my husband did this to me, and he will probably try it again."

The Doctor looked at me, but I'm not sure if he believed what I was saying. He told me John has been here all through my ordeal and has been very concerned about me. "Your very lucky to have him." He left the room and a nurse came in, and put something in the IV tube. I felt myself drifting off again, "Miim help me," I found myself saying out loud.

Hours later, I woke again to find John in the room.

"Hi Honey, the Doctor told me that you have been having it pretty rough. How are you feeling now?"

"John, tell me about the fire, how did it start?"

"Honey, don't worry about this stuff now. After you get well, I will tell you everything. The Doctors don't want you to get excited, so I have to wait until you are better. I promise I will tell you everything that happened."

"John, tell me, did you set the fire?"

"Angie, where did you get an idea like that? The Doctors said you will be very confused for awhile. They said you won't remember much that happened. You may even hallucinate, or maybe believe things that are not real for awhile. Don't worry, I will help you get things sorted out in your head."

"I remember things."

"No Honey, I did not set the fire. You know that I would never hurt you. I love you. Things will be okay after awhile."

"John, do you mean to tell me that I was not going to divorce you, and I didn't get captured by people from another planet and held for two and a half years?"

John laughed, "Where did you come up with all that stuff? Boy, I didn't know being in a coma could give you such a strange imagination."

"I had another daughter with him."

John laughed again, but to me it was not funny. It was real! I know it! He is trying to make me believe that I'm the one that is not in their right mind. He will probably get away with trying to kill me.

"Honey, you mean you had a kid by an alien from outer space? Angie, I know that you are confused, but come on, aliens from outer space? Don't you see you have been in a coma for several weeks? What you are saying is not real. I know it seems real to you, but after awhile you will forget all of this. Honey, don't tell other people this. They will think there is something wrong with you. They might want to have you committed or something."

Now I get it! John has a plan. He is very convincing. He can use this outer space affair to have me committed. Doesn't he remember that Grant and Carrie both know about this too?

When the nurse came in again, John told her about my being captured by aliens. He wanted to know if this is normal for someone that has been in a coma. He was making a joke out of it, or was he covering his tracks? It sounded to me like he is planning to have me committed if his plan fails.

"Well I never heard that one, but it would not surprise me," the nurse said, with a chuckle. "I've heard all kinds of things, and patients do actually think they're true."

"You see Honey, you were not kidnapped. All of this is because you hit your head and you were in a coma for so long."

No one believes me. John is preparing everyone just in case I get the idea to leave. When the nurse left, John followed her on out to the hall and I could hear them talking and laughing. When he came in again, he just said the Doctors think that things will get back to normal but it may take some time.

I decided to just go along with him for awhile. Once I talk to Carrie and Grant, I will expose him for the liar he is, and if it isn't too late, I will find Miim. Thinking about him gave me a warm, loving feeling. I didn't realize how much I do love him. I want him so much. As soon as I can I will make my escape. I will get my children, and go back to Cribaar with Miim.

"Well, maybe I am a little confused. I feel so funny, and I can't seem to think straight. John, do you think I can talk to Carrie? Can you have her to come up here? I want to have a phone put in my room. I think I could start getting myself well if I could start talking to the kids, my parents and friends."

"Honey give it another day or two, when the Doctors say it's okay to have a phone."

"Okay, thanks! Well can I at least have a visitor. I want to see Carrie. Please call her, and tell her that I am out of the coma, and I want to talk to her."

"Listen Honey, there is something I have to tell you. There has been an accident, and I'm sorry, Carrie didn't make it."

"No John, please no," I cried. "Carrie is my best friend, she can't die, I need her," I sobbed.

"Angie calm down, you can't get upset right now. I'm sorry, I know how much she means to you. I wasn't going to tell you yet, but I knew you would find out soon."

"What happened to her?" I screamed out. "What happened to her? What did you do to her?"

John ran out of the room and the nurse came in again and put something in my IV. Again, I went off to sleep. I had terrible dreams about someone trying to chase me through the park. When I looked around all I could see was large black holes. I knew something was in them but I couldn't make it out. Then I felt someone taking my hand. It felt safe. "Come back to me," the voice was saying. I didn't want to go back because I was afraid it was John. I didn't wake up until the next morning. John didn't come the next day at all, but one of the nurses told me that he called to check up on me.

"You're one lucky lady to have a man that cares for you so much," she said.

I asked her if he was upset with me, and she said the Doctor thought it would be best if he didn't come for a couple of days because I was getting too upset when he was around.

"We have to get your blood pressure down before we can release you," she said very concerned.

"He told me my best friend was killed while I was in a coma. That's why I was upset. I think he killed her. I tried to tell you he threatened me. I need someone to believe me. He will try it again."

"I heard about your friend. That's a hard thing to go through." She is still looking at me like I am the one that is making all of this up about my husband trying to kill me.

"Do you know how it happened?"

"Only what I read in the newspaper. Why don't you get some rest, and we can talk about it later."

"That's all I've been doing is resting, please, I'm okay now. I want to hear what happened to her."

"Okay, I will tell you, but if your blood pressure starts going up, I quit talking."

"I promise I'll be okay."

"Your house was on fire and there was a lot of smoke. Your friend was found in your bedroom. They say she died of smoke inhalation."

"What was she doing there? She wasn't there when I jumped out the window."

"I don't know, I thought she was visiting you and maybe tried to get you out, and didn't know where you were."

"Thanks for telling me."

When she was out of the room, I cried again. I didn't want anyone to see me upset because they would just put me out again so I tried to remain as calm as possible. *Carrie, what happened to you? Did John do this? I'm so sorry. He set the fire, I know it. That means he murdered you, and he will try to kill me again. Damn it, I wish they would stop giving me stuff that makes me sleep. I need to think. I have to figure a way out of here. Oh Carrie, Carrie, I can't stand the thought of being without you. Brian, poor Brian. He must be devastated. I've got to see him. I will have to get a hold of Grant as soon as I can. He will find out what happened to her. He knows all about Miim and Dani and how I feel about them. He will know how to get me out. He will help me find them. I must remain calm. That's the only way they will let me out of here. Oh Miim if you are near, don't you see I need you to take me away. I am so sorry that I didn't listen to you.*

The Doctor came in that night. He told me I was doing better. They would send me to x-ray in the morning and if that checked out, if I continue to improve, I could go home Friday. He warned me not to bump my head and to keep from getting upset. He then told me I was very lucky to be alive and the baby was okay. "You could have lost it."

"I'm pregnant?" I asked very shocked.

"Yes, between three and four months, you didn't know?"

"No, does John know?"

"Yes, we had to tell him because we had to run some tests. There was a chance that you could have lost it, and John signed the papers. We started prenatal vitamins in your IV. John has been very good, he said to do whatever it took to save you and the baby."

"I'm having a baby? Will it be alright Doctor?"

"After the fall you took, it is doing very well. We couldn't tell if it is a boy or girl yet. It was to soon during the time we ran the tests."

"How long is Friday? I don't even know what day it is."

"Day after tomorrow," I need to set up for your mental therapy and I need to see you back here in a couple of weeks."

"Why mental therapy?"

"Well you have been talking real strange so you will need to go for a while. At least until all this confusion goes away. Don't worry this is very normal for a person that has been through what you have been through. Also, I called in a pediatrician so you need to follow up on that to make sure your baby continues to do well.

Congratulations, I hear this will be your third," the Doctor said, smiling down at me.

"Yes, thanks!" I thought I had better not tell him about my baby from Miim. He might decide I needed to be committed to a mental hospital.

"I'm pregnant, oh wow, wait until Miim hears this. I can't wait to tell him. I'm going to have his baby. I was feeling so good about being pregnant that for awhile I could forget all the other problems. *I wonder what John is going to tell me. I wished he didn't know. He will probably tell me it's his, but I know that I haven't been with him for almost three years. How does he think he will get out of that one? I smiled to myself. I'm pregnant. I can get through this. I guess everyone thinks John is the father. Well maybe I can't blame them. I guess I would have thought the same thing if it were someone else.*

After getting this news, I was able to relax and my blood pressure started coming down. I knew I had to get well for the baby's sake. I was so excited about it.

The next day John came in. "I hear you get to come home tomorrow if all goes well," he said smiling.

"Yes, the Doctor said I will have to work on keeping my blood pressure down. I had an ex-ray this morning, and if it looks good, I might get to come home. I will have to have mental therapy for awhile. He says I have been confused, otherwise, I should mend very well. Did you know that we're going to have a baby?" I asked, more like a statement than a question.

"Yes, I was excited about it, but for awhile I thought you were going to miscarry. I wanted to be the one to tell you. I wasn't sure if you knew."

"No, I didn't know. Why didn't you tell me?"

"If things did not go right, I didn't want you to have to go through any more disappointment."

"Well I just found out, and I know that I have to take care of myself for the baby."

John came over to me and kissed me on the cheek. "That's my girl, I love you Honey. Everything is going to be just fine. I will get you the help you need. You will get over this idea, that you had planned to leave me for someone from outer space. You will be back to normal in no time, you will see."

After we got home on Friday, John took me up to the guest room. Although, I did a little walking while I was still in the hospital, I was still feeling quite dizzy.

"You can stay in here for a little while, at least until you fully recover. I will be right across the hall. I will take a couple of days off so that I can watch over you for awhile. No going up and down the steps without me, at least until we know that the dizziness is gone."

"Thanks," I said, but I was really hoping he would go on to work so that I could get out of here. Right now I could not trust him. He has been very nice, almost too nice. I thought maybe I should take advantage of it while it lasted. What else could I do? I just had to keep my guard up for now. At least, until I am well enough to take care of myself. I won't mention what I know about his affair with Kay. Maybe I can fake him out awhile and let him think I can't remember things.

"John, can we invite Grant over? I would like to see him. I want to talk to him about Carrie. There are some things I'm confused about. Maybe he can clear some things up for me."

"Sure Honey, I'll give him a call."

"There it was again, nice, too agreeable, but I did not want him to think that I doubted him. Not until I talked to Grant.

Later when he brought lunch up to me, he told me that Grant would be over tomorrow. He asked me if I was sure I was up to it. I told him that as soon as I can get things clear in my head I can start healing.

"John, will you tell me about the fire, how it started?"

"The fireman told me that it started in the kitchen. I guess you left the burner on, and there was some paper nearby."

Did he really expect me to believe that I would leave some paper near a gas stove?

"Where did you go, after we had an argument?"

"Angie, we didn't have an argument that day. I was on my way home when the fire started." He sat on the bed next to me, and put his arm around my shoulder. "I worked late that night. I was the one who found you on the ground when I got home, and called the ambulance. I thought you were gone. You looked so bad. At the time, I didn't know you were pregnant. I hate to think what could have happened to you or the baby. I'm the one that performed CPR," he said with tears in his eyes. "I wished I would have known that Carrie was inside or I would have gone in after her. I'm sorry that I didn't save her." He said this as he hung his head down and made short sobbing sounds.

What an actor, he almost sounded convincing. Did he really think I was going to believe all those lies? How did he know that I meant we argued the day of the fire. He said we didn't have an argument that day. Isn't that proof he is lying to me? He is working hard at trying to make me believe I'm the one that is crazy. Well I can act too, if need be.

"You attacked me, John. We were struggling and the phone rang. I got away from you, and I ran upstairs. Shortly after that there was smoke and you were gone. I screamed out for you to help me, John. You left me there to die, you didn't come back for me," I cried. At the same time, I remained calm.

"Angie, Honey, It didn't happen that way. You're very confused right now. If you tell people things like that it will make you look like you are losing your mind. People are not going to believe you. Your mind has had a chance to invent all kinds of things. Just talk to the therapist about this. He will get you through it. This will all go away, I promise. You will be fine." He stood up, looked down at me. He seemed very calm. His voice almost soothing. He walked over to the door and stopped. He turned around to me. He stretched out his arms, obviously hoping I would go to him, but I took a step back. I have already decided, if I could help it, he will never touch me again. If I have to use losing my mind as an excuse, then so be it.

"I need time John, I can't think. The coma made me have nightmares, and I feel so confused. I thought you were trying to kill me so I wouldn't run off from you again, and take the kids from you."

"You will be okay Honey, I will give you plenty of time to get this out of your mind. You'll come around, you'll see."

So why did he feel like he had to keep repeating himself?

"I'm sorry John, everything I told you seems so real to me. I feel dizzy and I just want to rest for now."

He went out of my room. I sat on the bed and put my hand across my belly, and thought. *Don't worry little one we will find your daddy. When Grant comes tomorrow he will confirm everything I said. John will not get away with this. We will expose him for the liar he is. He doesn't know that I went to Grant's office and told him more about what happened to me while I was missing. I am so glad that I have you little one.*

All I could do was stay in my room for now. I will pretend to believe everything that John told me. I need to make a plan on how to get the kids away from my parents. I don't think John will try to hurt me now but I will stay cautious. I will just remember to stay away from the steps while he is around. He knows he would be investigated if anything happens to me. If only I knew where Miim was. I need him to help me. I tried to calculate around the time that the space ship was suppose to leave but I just couldn't remember if there was a specific date. He could be gone. He probably couldn't wait any longer. I will not see my Dani for almost two years. I cannot stay with John for that long, nor could I live with my parents. Right now, I didn't know what I was going to do. I need a plan but first I just have to get better. *Please God I need help,* I cried.

That night I had horrible nightmares. I dreamed that John beat Miim as Miim was bending over me trying to save my life. My three children were watching and screaming. I could see blood running down Miim's face, but he still didn't stop CPR on me. My mind was telling me to get up but I could not get my body to move. I wanted to fight John off Miim, so that he could save me. I could see other people in the background but no one made a move to help us. Grant came forward, but said that John had every right to beat the man who took me away from him, so he did nothing to help. John started kicking Miim until he could do nothing to help me. Miim was laying on the ground, and I figured he died trying to save my life. I woke up screaming, my heart beating so hard I thought it was going to beat out of my chest. What if John killed Miim. I've been in a coma for the last six weeks. I don't know what happened in that time. John could have found out who he was and got rid of him. He would have gotten away with it because there is no Miim here. I felt myself panic and knew that I had to calm down for the sake of the baby. I want this baby even if I never see Miim again. I felt the baby moving for the first time and it made me relax a little. I got up, walked around, praying that I didn't wake John. I listened, but did not hear him. I went back to bed, thinking that Miim is strong, much stronger then John. Miim knew how to take care of himself. I thought of how I was going to get away from John. I knew that sooner or later, John was going to make a mistake, or I was going to find proof that he is lying. Somehow, I will have him put in jail for what he did to Carrie. I will get my children and leave.

I couldn't get back to sleep, so I laid there, thinking about the great time I had on Cribaar. It was hard to get use to at first. The people there were so much more advanced than us. I liked that they didn't use money. Everyone was equal and so much happier than we are. I thought about the warmth and love they had for each other, and how Miim liked to show me around. One day, when I was pregnant with Dani, we went out for a walk. He showed me some rocks that resembled marble. He told me they don't collect the stones because they are a part of their planet, and unless it is used to return to the planet, they leave them where they are. As he showed me things, he would pick up my hand and smile down at me, and watched me as I was in awe of my surroundings. He enjoyed watching me as much as I enjoyed his presence, and the beauty of everything around me. The animals there are about the same as on earth, but not as much of a variety. It was fun to watch the birds or the butterflies in the park. I wanted to be back there now and I wanted my children to be there. It was so much of a perfect world, and Miim is so much of a perfect love. I miss him terribly. Of course there are things we will miss here, but I knew that someday we would be able to come back. The last few months that I was on Cribaar, we were out walking and sight seeing almost every day. We would take Dani in her walker, and later we each held one of her tiny hands, and walk around the park. Her daddy would pick her up when she got tired. The weather was mostly warm, and some days we would get light showers. We would just stay home enjoying our child and each other until it was time to eat. We then, would spend time with friends and family. We loved going to the dining hall and watching all the new babies. Sometimes we would take turns in the nursery watching each others babies so that we could enjoy our meals and spend time with other couples. The men would join the women in the nursery when it was their turn. They believe children are both of their parents responsibilities. Miim enjoyed it as much as I did. He was so funny pretending to be a silly animal or reading and playing games with them. They would laugh so hard and he would get so tickled. A few days before we left, I found out that Ann and Deriff were going to have another baby and I prayed that she would be able to carry this one until full term. Since we were promised that we could come back for our children, we kept our plans. Ann had to stay behind for fear of losing the baby, but I promised her I would check up on her children. If they were in a bad situation, I would somehow get them. She told me they are probably living with her parents because her husband is, more than likely, busy with other women. She said she is sure he is glad to have her out of his way, and doubts that he even bothered to look for her. I took several pictures of her so that I can show her parents that she is happy. She also gave me a letter for them, with hopes to get her children. I thought about all of this now, and wondering how I was going to get to them when I can't even get my own children, without drawing suspicion. Where would I keep them until I can find Miim? I guess I can, at least find them and check up on them. Right now, I have to find out if the space craft is still here. I have to concentrate on getting myself well and taking care of this baby. Even if the spaceship is here I wouldn't be able to go back with them until the baby comes.

I thought to myself, how can I make up so much detail, if none of this is true? I am sure that I am right, and John is trying to make me feel like the coma has me making things up.

I smiled to myself, realizing, some day, I will find Miim again, or he will find me.

I had to think, what did I do with the pictures, and the letter that Ann gave me? If they were in my purse when the house caught fire, it means they might be destroyed, or John made sure they were.

After a while I was able to fall back to sleep, thinking of all the wonderful things about Cribaar, Miim, Andrew, Alyssa and Dani. Now, our new little person. Miim is going to be so excited. I can't wait to tell him. I hope I can give him another little girl.

CHAPTER NINE

John came up to my room the next morning with a tray of breakfast and coffee. He is still being extra sweet to me. He seemed to be in a very good mood. I thought he was playing the good husband part, very well.

"Good morning Honey," he said with a smile. This time he didn't come close to me, but I still did not trust him. "Grant will be over in a little while. Do you want to come down?"

"Yes, I want to walk around a little more and start getting some exercise." I said as I pointed to my stomach.

"Okay but you stay here. I will come get you. I don't want you to do the stairs by yourself yet."

I wonder what he is up to. I went through two pregnancies with him and he didn't lift a finger to help me. There was even a time when I had the flu and both kids were sick. My dear husband went off to work. When he got home I was cleaning after my sick children and was up all night with them. Still no help from him. He slept through it, and I was so sick, all I wanted to do was go to bed and get some sleep. Now he is just too nice for me to believe that he doesn't have a motive.

John went out of my room and I did try to eat some but I had a little bit of an upset stomach. I didn't eat much but I think secretly, I was not sure if I should trust him enough to eat what he makes. I don't think he would kill me now but he could try to get rid of the baby.

I tried to comb my hair but it was very short from them shaving me for the surgery. I hated the way I looked. I applied a little makeup but I don't think I improved the way I look. I kept my robe and slippers on and straightened my bed a little. About a half hour later, John came back for me.

"I will help you with your shower after Grant leaves," he said. "You shouldn't go on your own yet just in case you're still getting dizzy."

I hated that, but I knew he was right. I couldn't take a chance of falling again.

"Come on, I will take you down stairs. He will be here in just a little while. You didn't eat much of your breakfast. You have to stay strong for the baby."

"I will try to eat later. I'm feeling a little sick this morning," I said, as I walked toward John still a little dizzy. He reached for me to steady me. He then brought me into his arms and held me close to him.

"Looks like you're going to need me to stay with you a few more days then planned," he said smiling down at me.

I was getting uncomfortable in his arms, and I think he knew it. He grabbed me with his arm around my shoulder, and led me downstairs. I was feeling very nervous with him walking beside me. It would only take a small push. We just came down, and John had me to sit down when the door bell rang.

"Hi Grant, how have you been? It sure is good to see you."

"Hi Angie, gosh you look great. A lot better than when we last saw you. We were so worried."

"I'm fine now." I said as I gave him a hug. "I look terrible. I'm not use to having my hair this short." He took a seat next to me and I noticed he seemed a little nervous. At first he didn't say anything, and I wondered if he even wanted to be here.

"Grant I want to know what happened the night of the fire. What happened to Carrie?" I found it hard to contain my emotions but I had to know.

"There is a fireman's report stating the fire started in the kitchen. You left the stove on heating up some Chinese food. I guess it got hot, and ignited some sale papers that were on the table near by. The papers and the table caught fire." He said this as he crossed his leg, and looked up to John, as if he needed approval from him.

Why does he appear to be so nervous? I thought, *and why do I think he is about to lie to me?*

"Grant, I didn't turn the stove on. John came in from work, and he said that he was not ready to eat."

"Do you mean you remember what happened? The Doctors told me that it is unlikely that you would remember anything. We all thought you would never regain your memory."

"She thinks we had an argument and I attacked her," John jumped right in. I felt like he was making fun of me. "You remember Grant, the Doctor told us she would be very confused after being in a coma for so long."

"I'm not confused. I remember everything that happened before I jumped out the window. John tried to rape me. We got a phone call and I was able to push him away and run to my room. John set that fire. He wanted me dead." I cried.

"Angie, you need to stay calm. John told me last night that I have to stop if you get upset. John saved your life. He didn't want you dead. He was doing CPR when the PEDS arrived. I know what you are saying must seem so real to you, but don't you see how confused you are?"

I looked over at John, he appeared to be very hurt, but I had to go on. I had to know what was happening with these two.

"How did Carrie fit into the picture? Why is she dead?" I tried desperately to remain calm, so that he would not stop talking to me.

"Angie, getting excited will not make you well." John reminded me. "Maybe we need to talk about this another time Grant. I don't want her to be upset."

"No, please go on," I turned to Grant, and he seemed genuinely concerned.

"We don't know exactly what happened. We were hoping, eventually, you would remember and tell us. Near as we could figure you forgot about the stove. When Carrie came over and you were talking, I guess you went on upstairs for something. That's when you started smelling smoke. You jumped out of the window and Carrie, I guess, went up after you. She could not find you and she got trapped in the fire."

"Grant do you really think I would go on out the window if I knew Carrie was here? I would have found a way to save her. The smoke was getting heavy and I couldn't breath. I felt myself losing conscious. I knew I had to get out or die. You are saying Carrie came up to look for me, to get me out, and she went to my bedroom instead of the spare room, and she got trapped. I'm telling you Grant, that is not how it happened. Carrie was not there when I went upstairs, John was."

"I guess it is possible that Carrie came over, saw the smoke, and tried to get to you, but John was not home from work yet. He was seen coming home after the fire started. He is innocent."

"Who reported the fire?"

"Carrie did!"

"Grant, I remember every detail about the fire. I'm telling you, I didn't put food on the stove. I could not have started it. Not even by accident. Carrie was not here when the fire started. I didn't hear her when I jumped out the window. I was screaming for help, but I didn't hear anyone call for me. John was here, when I went on to bed. You have to believe me. It had to be him that set the fire." It was difficult to contain my emotions but I knew I had to get all of this out in the open. I also had to know what John did to Carrie and I had to know if there is a possibility that he would try to kill me again.

"Angie, we're not sure of all the details. You might be right about her coming later. At any rate, she called in about the fire and went in after you. That's when she must have gotten trapped. John came home from work and found you outside on the patio. You have to believe, he didn't know Carrie was here."

"Why do you think Carrie came over so late? Don't you think she suspected something was wrong when she called and John sounded strange to her? Why can't you believe me Grant? John attacked me that night and he set the fire. Why don't you tell him the truth John? Where were you when the fire started?"

"No Angie, John did not do anything wrong." Grant said this as he reached over and touched my hand. He shook his head back and forth, slowly, looking at me with pity. At this point I didn't know what to believe. *Maybe I am the one that is crazy. Maybe John did not do all of those things that I am accusing him of. In spite of what I believe to be true, there is a small chance that I am the one that is wrong.* John and I exchanged looks. He had an evil look, like I dare you to do this to me. I thought I had better back off.

"Thank you for saving me John," I looked at him with pleading eyes although I was still not convinced that he didn't try to kill me. I guess I will just have to pretend to make them believe that I am the one with the memory problem.

"I guess, because of the coma, my memory is playing tricks on me. I thought you were mad at me, because I told you that I was in love with the man that captured me. I am sorry John, I thought you wanted to kill me."

"What's that all about?" Grant said, looking a little perplexed.

"Oh yea, Angie thinks she was abducted by someone from out of space, and he forced her to have sex. She thinks she had a green baby or something. She also thinks she is in love with this alien," John said to Grant, making fun of the situation.

This made me even more angry at John, so I jumped right in. "Grant, I told you all about it the day after I got back. You're the one that wanted to know where I was for so long. You remember, you sat right there for over an hour, and listened to my story."

"Angie, we never had that conversation. You were not missing for two and a half years, or as far as I know you were not missing at all. I'm sorry but you have been in a coma for a long time. You are very confused. Don't worry, you are going to be okay."

"No, no, you're wrong. I'm pregnant, but this is not John's baby. This is Miim's baby. John and I have not made love in almost three years. Tell him John, that we haven't been together in almost three years. You're lying, you're both lying to me. I don't know what's going on here, but I intend to find out. This baby is real. Miim is real and planet Cribaar is real. I know it." I was yelling at them both, as I ran out of the room, and up the stairs. I noticed as I was getting out that John and Grant looked at each other, like the poor girl is crazy. John called after me, but I didn't stop.

Miim, I know that I am not making you up. Why are they acting like I'm crazy? Where are you Miim? I want to be with you now. We can go get the kids and run for it. I can't bear the thought of staying here any longer. I love you Miim, can you hear me. Please come get me. It was at that moment I thought about the disk on the key ring. *My purse, where is my purse? The disk is in there.* I looked around the room for my purse, but could not locate it. I ran to our bedroom that John and I had shared and franticly searched, but to no avail. When John came up to check on me after Grant left, I asked him where my purse was, but he was more concerned about my running up the stairs.

"Honey, you have to be careful about rushing around. You have to take it easy for awhile," he said, as he thrust his hands deep in his pockets. "You know what the Doctors told you. I guess your purse got burned up in the fire, I haven't seen it. Are you okay Angie?"

Oh no, what will I do now? I can't get in touch with Miim. What if it's been too long? Maybe he had to leave me after the fall. He probably doesn't even know that I was in the hospital. I wonder if he thinks that I didn't want to go back with him and I just ignored him? Oh Miim, I may never see you again, and even if you come back I will not see Dani until she is almost four. I will miss part of her growing up, like I missed Andrew and Alyssa. Andrew and Alyssa, I want to see them. They knew I was missing, and so did my parents. They will tell me the truth, or at least my children will. I understand why John is lying to me. He wants to save himself, but why would Grant lie about it? Why is he taking up for John? I feel so dizzy.

"What is it Angie, what's wrong with you? You look like you've seen a ghost. You know you can't go running up the stairs like that yet. Was there something in your purse that was important? Don't worry, I will get you a new credit card and your new license are already on the way."

"I remember now John, I remember, I left my purse downstairs. I tried to find it the day of the fire and I remember I panicked because I couldn't find it. Where is it John?"

"I don't know what you are talking about Angie. I have not seen your purse. You have got to stop driving yourself crazy or you will only get worse. Look at you, you're shaking all over. Come on let's get you into bed.

Here, take one of these pills the Doctor gave you, and please try to calm down. Stop thinking of these crazy ideas. Do you want me to stay with you?"

"No, I am feeling better. I will be okay after I get some rest. John can we go up to see the kids next weekend?"

"Sure Honey, if you are feeling up to it, we will go. I'll go get you a cup of tea and something to help you relax. I want you get some sleep. Maybe you will wake up feeling better. I don't want Grant thinking that I have treated you badly."

"I'm sorry, I feel like I'm taking too much medication. I need to think more clearly. I'll call Grant tomorrow and set him straight. I miss the kids terribly. Thanks for taking me to see them."

He walked out of the room, and I was aware that he did not mention at all about being careful because of the baby. I know he does not want it, and I think I will ask him about it. Then it suddenly came to me. Why would he order a new credit card and license unless he knew the old ones got burned up in the fire? There was not that much damage in the living room down stairs. I'm sure that is where I left my purse. It would not have burned up. So what did he do with it? I will watch him carefully. He will make other mistakes, and I can prove that he is lying. I am not as sick as they are making me out to be. I wonder what he did with the disk that was in it. It was attached to my keys and I'm sure he had no idea what it was. It looked like a small light. I looked around the room. Nothing looked the same as I remembered. New wood, new paint, even the furniture was new. I walked over to the window where I jumped. I wondered where I fell. I felt sick to my stomach. What would I have done if I knew I was pregnant? Would I have jumped out the window?

John returned with the tea and another pill that I did not recognize. I only pretended to take it. I wanted to keep my mind clear and I didn't want to take any medicine, unless I had to because of the baby. He put his hand over mine, and I felt myself cringe from his touch.

"You will be okay, just get some rest. We can get that shower later. I will call the Doctor to see if he agrees that you can travel." He almost sounded like he really cared, but I think he wanted to tell the Doctor about my being upset. I'm sure he wants to cover his own tracks.

The following week-end, we took the long drive up to see the children. Even though I didn't trust him, he was the only way that I was going to see my children. On the way up, John was telling me again all the things that he wanted us to do as a family. He said he couldn't wait until things got back to normal.

"Angie, I almost lost you and I want to do whatever it takes to get us back on the right track. I know that I haven't given you and the kids the attention you need. I dropped my gym membership and I cut my hours back at work so we can be a family. What do you think about that?"

I wasn't sure what to think, why couldn't he have done that before? I still didn't believe anything he said.

"I'm not sure John, I don't even know who I am anymore. I keep thinking about things that everyone says is not real, but they seem real to me. Right now, I feel like Grant is lying to me and you are lying to me. After I talk to the kids and my parents, I will get things straight in my head. John can't we bring the kids home?"

"Not yet, Honey! Your Doctors don't think you are ready."

"What about this baby? Are you sure you want me to stay around with another child on the way? You didn't even ask about it last night when I was upset. You made it very clear to me before, that you did not want another child."

"I told you, Angie, I am happy about it now that you are pregnant. I just didn't think we should have another one the last time we talked about it. I admit we were having some problems, but I want to fix them. I want to focus on our marriage and the kids. I have changed my mind. Of course I want this baby."

"What if it is not yours? Do you still want us to keep it?" I stared ahead of me but I didn't feel like saying anything else.

"The baby is mine you will remember soon. Please don't say it belongs to someone else, especially to your parents. You know they will only take my side on this. It will be okay, you'll see," John said, as he reached over to pat my leg. I thought I detected a sharp tone to his voice.

We got to my parents about another hour. The kids both ran up to me, and they wanted to hug me but John told them to be careful, that I still had some pain.

After greeting them, and my parents, I went to the living room to relax a bit. The kids followed me. They had so many questions. John sat next to me. Usually he went off somewhere with my father, but I felt like he wanted to see what I was going to say to the kids, or more like, what they were going to say to me. He stayed right beside me watching over me. My father and mother also came in. I couldn't help to notice how much my father had aged, and how much thinner he became in just a couple months since I have seen him.

"We were at the hospital a couple of times while you were there," my mother announced. "We were so worried about you. Tell us about it. The Doctors told us you probably wouldn't remember anything."

"I remember a lot, at least I guess I do. Everyone keeps telling me that I'm all confused. Would you believe I thought I got captured and held against my will for over two years. Does anyone remember my telling them anything like that? No! Well Andrew, why don't you tell me what you remember?"

"I mostly remember about, you were in a fire and hit your head." I thought he glanced at me too quickly and looked away. "I'm glad you are okay mom."

"Do you remember my being here after I got captured. That's when I hadn't seen you or Alyssa for two and a half years?"

"Well Daddy says that you never got captured. He says you hit your head, and you were in a coma for a long time. He just said you have been confused and you won't remember anything before the fire."

"Okay, Mother, do you think I disappeared before I was in the fire?"

"Well, I know that you think you did, but don't worry honey, you will get better, and you will remember what really happened. Look, I will make us some nice dinner. You just relax dear, Alyssa and Andy will help me."

"Why is everyone evading the issue? Why can't I hear the truth of what really happened? Dad, you tell me what happened before the fire."

"All I know is you were here before the fire. Nobody ever told me what you did before that happened. Come on John, I want to show you my trophy. I caught the largest bass in the local tournament."

"Alyssa, do you remember telling me that you prayed for me while I was gone, you remember, when I was missing all that time?"

"Yes Mommy, I prayed that you would get better. I missed you cause you were in the hospital sick."

Okay, now I get it, John told them to keep it quiet. He told the kids that I have been confused and I was not captured and he probably told my parents that I cracked up and I just think that I got captured. Not a one of them believe me, or am I the crazy one around here. Maybe I have been crazy for a long time. That would mean there is no Miim, no Dani in my life. There is no planet Cribaar. Oh Miim, I can't stand not ever being with you. I couldn't have made you up. You are too real to me. I can't have feelings like this for someone that does not exist. We made love, it was too wonderful for it to be made up. I can still feel you in my heart. Miim, please come to me, I love you. I can't be without you. I'm getting dizzy again, oh help me Miim. The baby, I have to be careful, I can't lose this baby.

That's the last I remember until I woke up screaming during the night. I was having dreams about John killing Miim again. The dreams were so vivid. I dreamed that John had a gun and when he saw me with Miim he shot him. He then turned the gun on me, and was about to shoot me and he saw that I was pregnant. He asked me who the father was, but I told him I didn't remember. I knew he would kill me and the baby if he knew. That is when I woke up. I didn't remember screaming, but John told me that I did. He came to me, and gathered me up in his arms, holding me, and telling me everything would be okay.

"I'm sorry, Honey, I'm sorry that you are so confused. Tell me what you were dreaming."

"John, what did you do with Miim?" I asked.

"With who? Oh yea, he's the guy that you think captured you. Honey, I didn't do anything to anyone."

"You shot him, didn't you?"

"Honey, it was a dream, a very bad dream. Here take one of these pills, it will help you to calm down."

Why is it that he kept me drugged up with pills. He wants me to be confused. He doesn't want me to remember anything that happened. About this time my mother was standing over us with a worried look on her face.

"She'll be alright, Myra," John said as he rocked me back and forth like I was a baby. I will take her to the Doctor Monday. Maybe he can give her something."

I *don't want anything else*. I was screaming inside. *I just want him to leave me alone*.

"What about the baby? Will it be Okay?" Myra appeared concerned.

"You told her about the baby?" I asked, "I thought we should do that together."

"Well your mom kind of guessed after you passed out, so, I told her that I was going to be a father again." He looked at Myra with pity for me and I almost believed his concern. "Don't worry, I will get her an appointment. Listen, you go get some sleep. I will sit with her. She has been under a lot of strain. I guess I shouldn't have made this trip yet."

Mother went on back to bed, and John just sat there with me in his arms, stroking my hair.

"John, I'm sorry. Right now I don't know what's real, and what's not. I know that you didn't kill Miim. My dreams feel so real to me."

"I know Honey, and this will get better, I'm sure. Now you lay down here on the sofa. I will get you a cup of tea. I'm sleeping right here beside you in case you need me. I'm worried about your passing out like that."

"I'm sorry John, I don't mean to worry you."

After going back to bed John curled up next to me, with his arm across my waist. I felt uncomfortable with him being so close, but I just had to endure his presence. There was nothing to do, nothing else to say. I only had my wonderful thoughts about my other family on Cribaar. I closed my eyes so John would think that I needed the rest. I thought about Dani. I took myself back to the day she was born. Of course she was a beautiful baby. I could see a lot of Miim in her. That beautiful little dimpled smile, such a good baby. I had a hard time in the delivery room. It was a very long labor and I had a lot more bleeding than normal. Even the Doctors were worried and all I could think of was when Ann lost her baby. Miim held my hand, and wiped the tears from my eyes and sweat from my forehead. He looked so worried. The Doctors tried several times to get him to leave the delivery room, but he insisted he would stay with me. During my pregnancy he was so worried about my losing weight but Doctors assured him that my weight loss had nothing to do with the baby's weight. I just felt very sick most of the pregnancy. I could not hold down food very well, no matter what Miim tried to get me to eat. At one point, I told him that I knew he would take very good care of the baby if anything ever happened to me. He had tears in his eyes as he told me he didn't want me to ever think that again. He said he couldn't stand it if he lost either one of us. After she finally arrived, we figured her earth weight to be about six pounds. Miim held her and kissed her cheek several times. Then he came over and kissed my cheek. He looked so cute with a baby in his arm, holding her ever so gentle.

"I was so worried about you."

"I know!"

"We will never go through this again. Dani is our only child together, yes?"

"But Miim, you said you wanted more children."

"Yes, that was before I knew that it was going to be this hard on you. Angie, I thought I was going to lose you, and I can't take another chance like that. Dani needs her mom and so do I."

"I'm okay, the next one will probably be easier. Honest Miim, I am fine. The Doctors said it was a tough delivery, but I will be okay."

"We'll see how strong you will be. I don't think I could ever go through this again either. Thank you for the most precious gift you could give me," he said sweetly. "I love my two girls."

"Thank you for talking me into it," I said, although I felt very tired. "I wish I could have a picture of you two right now. I want to capture this moment."

"That can be arranged. Here take her. I will get Dad to take a picture."

Back to reality, I said, "John, I had a couple of pictures, did they get burned up in the fire?"

"Pictures, what pictures?"

"Pictures of me, Miim and Dani, did you ever see them? I had them in my purse."

"No Angie, I didn't see any pictures. Listen you have to get over this, so you can get on with your life. If you keep believing and thinking about this stuff, you will never get over it. Nothing you are saying makes sense. You are carrying my child, understand." John sounded irritated, and rolled over away from me.

"Yes John, I understand. When did we make love? I'm sorry, I just don't remember."

"Plenty of times before you got hurt. I wished we could have waited until you were well to have another baby, but I would have agreed. I almost lost you Angie, and right now I feel very close to you. I just want everything to be right between us."

Maybe, what he is saying is the truth, and I am carrying his child. I really don't believe that but I have to think of it as a possibility. I feel that he is lying to me. I remember putting the pictures in my purse. Why do I remember everything, down to the last detail of delivering my last child? If I have a bad memory of what really happened, I sure have a good imagination. If I did make all this up in my mind, that means that I am going to have to make the most of my marriage for the children's sake. I will have to move back in my bedroom with John, and try to love him again, but how? Especially when I feel that he wanted to kill me. I need to prove it to myself that I have been living in a fantasy world, or do I need to prove that everything that I believe is real? Why do I have the feeling that John wants to control me? I need to think! He again rolled over toward me and put his arm around me and gathered me up to pull me even closer. He kissed me on the cheek and then my lips. There was no where for me to go, so I just endured his pretense of affection. At least he didn't push love making for now.

CHAPTER TEN

After saying good by to my parents and the children, and reassuring everyone that I would be okay, John and I left for home. Even my father seemed concerned about me. I was not looking forward to the long trip. I didn't feel like talking, but I wanted to get John's response about his affair with Kay.

"That didn't happen, you are dreaming again," he said vehemently.

Why are you angry with me? I'm just trying to sort things out in my mind."

"I would not cheat on you Angie, and we're not going to discuss this any longer. You have to get over this stuff that's going on in your head. In a couple of days you will see Dr. Newman and he will help you sort out what's real or not. For now I want you to drop it."

"You say you want to work things out between us. How are we suppose to do that if I don't ask you questions? I'm trying to remember."

"I'm sorry, I just keep thinking you're trying to find excuses to end our marriage. I'm trying to make things work."

"I know, just be patient with me. John, do you think I'm beautiful?"

"Of course you're beautiful, you know I think you are."

"You just never told me that."

The rest of the trip we remained silent, but I couldn't help wondering why he was angry instead of laughing it off. It just gave me more reason to believe that he did have an affair.

As soon as we got home he walked with me upstairs and asked me if I needed anything. His back was against me, as he slowly walked away saying he loved me. I don't know why he said it while walking away but he did sound sincere.

"You and the kids are my world and I will do what it takes to make you love me and trust me again. I'm glad that you are home from the hospital. You just don't know what I've been through these past few weeks not knowing if you were going to come out of the coma. I didn't have a lot of hope that you would be completely well. Don't you see, I almost lost you." He turned around to me. He had tears in his eyes.

He sounded so sincere. I've never seen tears in his eyes and I was feeling guilty. "Give me time John, I will try. We do need to talk about all the things going through my head without you getting angry with me. I can't sort these things out on my own."

"I know, I'll go get something to help you sleep," he said, as he was making a quick exit from the room.

I did not take the pills that John brought, out of concern for the baby.

That night I dreamed again, and again my dreams were so vivid. I could hear Miim calling me. I felt myself reach up to touch him, but he was backing up. He was begging me to come with him. I couldn't touch him. He was too far away. I was crying and begging him not to leave without me. He was telling me that this was my last chance. If I didn't come now he would have to leave me. He started to fade away and I kept calling out to him. I could hear him say he will always love me. He faded more and more and then he was gone. "Miim, Miim," I shouted. I woke up. I was pouring with sweat. I didn't know if I called out loud or not, but I didn't hear John come so at least I didn't wake him. I laid there and thought about Miim. Could I have made him up? I know every curve in his face, his dimples and the exact shape of his nose. He has to be real. Could being in a coma invent this man down to the last detail? I really don't think so. My feelings for him are too strong. If John is lying why would Grant go along with his lies? None of it makes since to me. I also wondered if Miim gave up on me, or chose someone else to go back with him. It would be my fault. I should have trusted him when he wanted me to get the kids, and run for it. He wanted to help me, but I had to do it my way. I got myself into this mess now I have to figure a way out. It's hard to believe John was capable of killing me. Even more so now that he seems to love me. His tears were genuine. How can I stay with him when I am in love with someone else? If I knew for sure he was having an affair it would be easier to leave. I have to find out if what John was saying is true. Maybe I never was missing for so long, or he never had an affair, but, how will I find out? I cried myself back to sleep as my mind kept racing from one thing to the next.

The next day John called the Doctor's office, and they told him to bring me in that day. When we got there, John followed me back to the examining room. I was glad when Doctor Shinsor asked him to wait outside while he examined me. He assured him, that I was in good hands.

The Doctor was a very soft spoken man, a little on the heavy side for a Doctor. His high pitched voice did not seen to match his body. He was in his mid forties, not bad looking, although balding slightly. He looked at me with worry wrinkling his forehead. He had soft brown eyes and I believed I could tell him anything.

"What's going on with you?" he asked, as soon as John was out of sight.

"Everyone tells me that you ran some tests on this baby while I was in the hospital, but Doctors at the hospital told me the baby is doing fine. John insisted I come to you, rather than Dr. Vaughn, that delivered my other children. He said you would know about the tests that were done at the hospital. Is my baby okay Doctor?"

"The baby is doing fine, I'm talking about you Angie."

"I don't know, what did John tell you?"

"He just said that you have been talking crazy ever since you have been out of the hospital and that you have been having bad dreams. He said you keep getting dizzy, and you passed out, also you scream out in the night. He is very concerned about you and the baby."

"I guess when I jumped out the window, and hit my head, I thought someone abducted me, and took me to some where strange. I thought I was forced to have a child with him. To tell you the truth Doctor I thought this really happened before the fall, but John said I'm confused, and I was not missing. I know I have been having weird dreams but everything else seems so real. I know that I was in a coma but could I have made all this up. I believe John started that fire when I jumped out of the window. I think he is responsible for my best friend's death."

"It's not unusual. You had a very bad concussion, and head trauma. Some people who have been in a coma for as long as you were, try to come back, but some are more comfortable where they are and do not want to come back. You are very lucky that you remember who you are. Some people have brain damage and never remember. Nightmares are not uncommon. Give yourself some time. They will probably fade away. I am more concerned about your passing out. I want to do a complete blood work-up and we will take a look at the medicines that you are taking.

"I haven't been taking the medicine. I don't trust John and I don't want to take the chance of hurting the baby. Can you guarantee that won't happen?"

"No guarantees but it is the same medicine that you were taking in the hospital. It is the mildest form of anti-seizure medicine that we have. It will help you relax and maybe even remember some things. Your blood pressure is out of control and this could cause you to lose the baby. Take the medicine, Angie."

"Doctor, I believe with all my heart that I was kidnapped, and missing for over two years. I'm telling you this because, if this did happen, then I had another child with this man and I almost lost it. I almost died, and I remember getting so dizzy. I even passed out on few occasions. They wanted to give me a blood transfusion, but where we were, they could not find a match."

"I remember reading about a bunch of women that were missing."

"How long ago Doctor?"

"Two maybe three years ago, I don't know, I'm not sure it has anything to do with you or maybe that incident had something to do with you believing it was you. Your mind can play tricks on you."

"Isn't it possible that I was one of those women. I remember so many details but John and the police tell me that I was never missing. How can that be?"

"It's hard to tell at this point Angie. You have an appointment with Dr. Newman soon. Talk to him about this and maybe he can give you an idea of what is going on. It would help me to know if you did have a dangerous pregnancy. At least I would know the signs and if you are at risk of losing this one."

"Doctor, I need to get proof. If I can prove that this is all a dream or result of a coma then I can let it go and go on with my life. Is it possible to do a DNA on an unborn baby?"

"Angie, what are you trying to say?"

"I'm trying to tell you that I don't think this baby is John's. If I did get captured, than it might be that someone else fathered my baby. I don't remember John and I being together for years. Wouldn't I have remembered that much, when I can remember so many other details? It just doesn't fit."

"Does John know this?"

"I told him but he doesn't believe me."

"Who do you want to be the father?"

"The person that captured me."

"Angie, you had better let this go. If what you are telling me is true and if John is willing to raise this baby as his own, consider yourself very lucky. You did your part by telling him what you think is the truth. That's all that is necessary. I had a chance to get to know John while I was running some tests at the hospital. He was very concerned about you and the baby. He called every day to find out if the test results were in."

"What if I told you that I didn't want to stay with John?"

"Angie you have to get yourself well and have this baby. You don't need any more stress. Maybe later you can think of what you will do. Right now, you need the medical insurance and you have to take care of yourself. Your blood pressure is high. If you want to stay pregnant until term, you should be thinking how your going to get through this pregnancy without losing the baby. You need to drop all these other things for now. We can not do a paternity test until after the fifth month. Right now you would be putting your baby at risk. Think about it before you make that kind of decision."

"I see you have been talking to John."

I knew he was right. He didn't want me to go any further with this, so for now, I will have to stay with John, get my children, and try to make things right. I could have a DNA later on and that would get rid of any doubts that I have. I knew that I had to stop thinking about Miim and our wonderful little girl. If the Doctor knew anything more he wasn't telling me. How could he not know that it was me that was missing? Unless I wasn't missing! Doctor Shinsor told me the baby was doing well. He also told me I have to focus on things that would make me relax, and get plenty of bed rest. He said he would talk to John and let him know that he needed to pamper me.

The next day was Tuesday, and my driver's license finally came. John told me he would not give them to me until he knew that I was completely well. I wanted to go to the library to do a newspaper search about the missing women, but I didn't want John to know. I had to be certain that one of them was me, and I just had to wait it out. I had to pretend that I didn't believe I was captured for now. I also decided not to talk about the fire. I needed to make sure this baby would be okay. John was very sweet to me, kissing me on the cheek, and patting my stomach every now and then. We talked about getting the kids soon. I knew he thought things were getting back to normal. John was taking me back to the Doctor once a week, and I worked at keeping my spirits up. My blood pressure improved, along with the dizziness. I was taking the medicine and feeling so much better.

The following month I asked John if we could have visitors.

"I think we should have Brian over. I haven't had a chance to tell him how sorry I am about Carrie."

"I think that would be a good idea, honey," John was surprisingly, very agreeable.

"He must be grieving terribly," I said very concerned.

"He is back to work and seems to be doing very well. I sent flowers and a card. I will call him in a week or two and invite him over. I didn't get to the funeral but I think he understands that I needed to be at the hospital. Let's concentrate on getting you completely well. Dr. Shinsor called me this morning and told me your blood pressure is a lot better, and your blood test are almost normal, but you are to still take it easy."

"I'm glad that you took care of things John, thanks. I am feeling a lot better. I would like to start cooking again. Maybe get out a little and do some grocery shopping."

"Maybe next week, let me talk to the Doctor. Honey, something is weird. I got our credit card bill, and it looks like someone got a hold of our number. Funny though, they only used it for small purchases and I know it couldn't have been you, because you have been in the hospital and I have been with you every day since you've been out."

"That's strange, what kind of items?"

"Just food, diapers, stuff like that."

"Well it sounds like a poor person that doesn't really want to steal, but maybe needs food. They obviously have a baby. I would let it go."

"Yea, I'll let it go, but I want to alert the credit card company. I should tell them to let me know before approving a large purchase. I'll order us some dinner. You are looking so much better today, Honey."

"Thanks, I'll go get a shower and call the kids while your picking up dinner." I walked out of the kitchen, and toward the steps, when I came to a complete halt. *Miim, it's Miim, I know it is. He is real, I knew that I wasn't making this up.* When we got back to earth, I gave him all the money that I had in my purse just in case they ran out of supplies. I also gave him one of my credit cards. I only had about a hundred dollars cash so he must have spent that. The date, I've got to find out the date that he used the card. I stood there thinking for the next few minutes and then slowly walked back into the kitchen. John was just getting off the phone.

"Could I see that bill, John?"

"You don't have to worry about it. I contacted them and they reassured me they would let me know if there is any large purchases."

"I was just curious. It will give me something to think about to get my mind off other things."

"Okay," he pulled the bill out of a drawer where he had just put it, and handed it to me.

"I'm going to get my shower, I'll get it back to you," I said smiling.

He shrugged his shoulders as he went out the door.

I looked at the bill, the last purchase was almost a month ago, but it did not prove he was still here. He probably ran out of money and when I got hurt he could not get any more. He used the credit card. I need more proof that he is real, but it did give me more hope. At least he knows that I was hurt. He will come back for me. He probably doesn't know that we are going to have another baby, or maybe he does.

I calculated that they were suppose to leave about two months ago, but stayed an extra month, maybe, waiting for me. He would be back. *Alright, I think I can deal with this. I can wait twenty months. I wished I could have seen*

Dani before they left. My sweet little baby girl. Miim will take good care of her. I wondered what Miim knew about the fire and my accident. *Poor Miim he must have been going out of his mind.*

I got in the shower, and as the warm water hit my face, my mind went back again to Miim. He talked me into getting under the water falls, and I was a bit frightened at first, but he reached out his hand to me and gently walked me in. The falls were so beautiful coming down over colorful rocks. The sky was just a bit different than ours, a little darker blue and sometimes a slight greenish and yellowish tint to it. Miim splashed me teasingly, and before it was over we were in a full fledged water battle which ended up in a romantic kiss. It's times like this, I can think back, and it will keep me going until he returns. Why did I ever let him go? Why didn't I tell him that I would go back with him, when my heart knew I would?

I heard the bathroom door open which brought me back to reality. John is back already? Why is he coming into the bathroom? I tried to pull the shower curtain around my body, and look out.

"Oh it's you," I said to John, as he came closer to me. "You frightened me, I thought you left."

"I did but I forgot to kiss you good by," he said smiling. I knew what he wanted. I knew that he could see my bare back side, and he was eyeing me up and down, with lust.

"John, I need another day or two, please let's not rush this, we will have plenty of time."

"Angie, I need you now," he said, almost in a whisper. He took a step closer and I was feeling like a trapped animal. He ran his hand down my wet arm, that was still holding the shower curtain, next to my body. I shuddered, thinking how I'm going to get out of this. His hand came down over my wet body. He knew I was frightened but it did not stop him.

"John, Dr. Shensor said, I still need to take it easy for awhile and get plenty of bed rest. Tomorrow I will see Doctor Newman. I am still feeling a bit dizzy, but if he says that is normal, and gives us the okay, then I will concentrate more on you and I, getting back what we had. Just wait until tomorrow. One more day, I want to be sure, okay Honey?"

"Okay, tomorrow!" He turned around and swiftly left the bathroom. I could tell that he was angry with me, but I felt relieved. I shivered from head to toe, although the water was warm. All I could think was, how I was going to keep from making love to my husband. Sooner or later I might have to give in to him, unless I can find out that he has been lying to me. *I've got to get to the library soon.* I thought, as I was trying to calm down.

John avoided me the rest of the day until dinner time. He brought me up some spaghetti and salad. He told me he would be going back to work in a few days. He also said after tomorrow he would drop me off for my appointments, and I could take a cab back until he gave my license back to me. I mostly stayed in my room the rest of the night, reading and watching television and making plans for going to the library as soon as he goes back to work.

That night I had another bad dream. I dreamed that I had my baby, and it was a girl, but no one could find her. The nurses kept telling me that John was the last person to see her, and they think he took her. I wanted to get up to find her, but they kept telling me that I needed to go back in a coma. I kept hearing John's voice, but I could not see him. He was telling the nurse that I will never see my baby until I can be a good wife and mother. I could hear my baby crying, and I screamed at John to give her to me. He said that she belonged to him and she was not mine. Then I saw him carry her away, only I could not see the baby. John's back was toward me and he was walking away. I could see that she was wrapped up in a blanket large enough to hang on the floor. When I woke up in a sweat, choking on my own saliva I was shaking all over. I put my hand to my stomach to make sure the baby was still there. It was too early to feel much movement yet, but I knew it was there. John will never see this child. He doesn't care about me or this baby. I've got to get out of here. I've got to find a way to get in touch with Miim. Most of all I've got to calm down for the sake of my baby. I couldn't help but wonder if John was putting something in my food or drinks to keep me drugged, or maybe even get rid of the baby. I wondered if he thought I was not taking the medicine and maybe putting more in my food. I thought about Carrie, he didn't seem that concerned about her death, or Brian's grieving. I just don't trust him, and I'm glad he is going to work. I will find out what happened, but tomorrow I have a Doctors appointment and John will be watching me. He will call me about the time he thinks I should be home. I will have to wait at least another week before getting to the library. I have been feeling trapped for too long. I felt that I needed to get out.

CHAPTER ELEVEN

I saw Doctor Newman the next day. He already had a file on me, studying it, as I walked in his office.

"So you are Angela Marcus?" he asked in a nice caring way as if I were a celebrity. "I've heard so much about you." He stood as he introduced himself and then took his seat, motioning me to sit down. He looked up at me, and then down at my files as if I didn't match what was in them.

"Yes, it's nice to meet you Doctor. Sorry I have not heard much about you."

I made up my mind before coming in that I would tell him the truth right from the beginning to the end. If he doesn't believe me then I will fake it from there. Someone, somewhere is going to have to believe me. I told him this before beginning, and he told me to let him be the judge of that. I instantly liked him and whatever I told him, I felt, he would not judge me. He seemed like a caring person. I liked his looks. A medium built man with soft eyes and a nice face. He had some graying around the temples which told me he was around fifty. He had a way about him that made you feel comfortable and he smiled a lot.

"First, I want to know if you have ever met my husband or spoken to him."

"No, I have not, he called to set the appointment but that is all." He leaned back in his chair with his arms behind his head. "Why don't you tell me a little about yourself, and why you think you are here."

"Okay, I begin by telling him a little about my marriage. I went on about getting kidnapped and about Miim, trying not to leave out details. I let him know I was doubting myself since I woke up from the coma. I went on about how hard it was to believe it didn't happen to me, and how real it feels. It felt so good getting the truth out. I haven't told this much about my experiences since I confided in Carrie. He didn't say one word the whole time I was talking. He was just letting me rattle on and on. I know the whole story sounded made up. I almost felt ridiculous telling it, but I knew I had to trust someone.

"I don't expect you to believe all this happened to me Doctor. I don't know if I believe it so I won't expect you to. I just feel in my heart that what I'm telling you is real. I just don't know if I can trust John, and that scares the hell out of me. He is trying to control me. He may even be drugging me. I keep having these weird dreams. I don't know where to go from here. I don't want to stay home. I just want Miim to be real, and for him to come for me and my children. I think it's funny that I remember so much detail, but what John doesn't want me to remember, he blames on the coma. He says this baby is his but yet I don't remember us sleeping together for almost three years.

After a long pause, when I realized my time was about up, he said, "That's some story. I guess if nothing else you could write a book about it."

"But what do you think Doctor? Am I crazy?"

"I'm not here to judge you, just to make evaluations. Let me go over this recording again, and I will give you more information next week. I can tell you what I do remember. There were a lot of women missing a few years ago, but nobody ever knew what happened to them. I didn't see anything in the paper about them being found, but I was on vacation several weeks ago."

"Don't you see the reason they didn't make it public could be because they would have to tell the truth. I don't think anyone wants the truth to be told, including the police."

"Well if what you remember is the truth then I can understand why the truth can not be told. Angie can you hold on to what you know for now?"

"Sure Doctor! John is not going to let me drive until I get your okay. I want to go to the library as soon as possible. Can you let him know that I can drive?"

"Oh, I don't see any reason why you can't drive in about a week if you don't get dizzy before then."

"Thank you Doctor, also John thinks that I should be ready to be his bed partner. I don't feel right about it."

"I can't help you there, but if you are still getting dizzy you should still take it easy for awhile. He needs to give you a little more time."

That evening at dinner time, I told John about the session and also that I will be able to drive in about a week if I don't get dizzy in the meantime. I also told him the Doctor said I need a little more time before we completely get back to normal. John had me over a barrel, and I knew that he would not give me my license until I was back in his bed.

"Good, that's great Honey. I talked to him today and he told me to give you at least another week before we make love. I want us back together as soon as possible." He picked up my hand and smiled. "One more week, huh?"

Oh, no, I thought, *how am I going to keep from this happening?* I just want to find other proof that Miim and Dani are real. Maybe eventually I can come to terms with reality, but not now. I will just have to find other ways to avoid John's advances. He knows that all the other Doctors gave the okay except for Dr, Newman. I feel like I would be cheating on Miim. I will get to that library and do a research as soon as I can. Right now John seems to be watching my every move.

"Maybe next week, after seeing Dr. Newman," I said to him as sweet as I could.

All the next week I was able to avoid John, although he has been very loving and nice, almost too nice. He has been very patient with me and spending as much time as he could with me. He has been bringing take out food home every day, and he hired a house keeper to do the chores. He has been calling me daily to check up on me, but I believe he wanted to make sure I stayed home. My suspicion of him only grew.

The following week I went to see Dr. Newman again and I brought him up to date. I told him how sweet John has been to me, and I thought it was because he wants me back in his bed tonight.

"I am still not ready for him."

"Angie, be careful," he said in a very concerned manner that almost chilled me. I believe something happened to you. I can't tell you if all the details you are telling me are true, but I believe you suffered some trauma before your fall. I think it's more than marriage failure."

"Doctor, do you mean you believe me?"

"Well, it's not whether I believe everything you said to be true, but I believe you think everything you told me is true. If that is the case than John may be dangerous. I pulled out all of your hospital reports and studied them. Since our session last week, I met with a medical team. Together, we made an evaluation. You are not crazy. Trauma can do funny things that seem real and sometimes patients have a hard time trying to decide what is real or not. You gave me so much detail, and yes, I do believe that some of what you told me is true. I think John did rough you up or may even caused your accident. The next session I want you to tell me everything again. We will break it down and you can tell me what you are sure is real and what is vague. For now just be careful. If John did make an attempt on your life, he could do it again. You would be better off agreeing with everything he says or does even if he wants you in his bed. Just find your proof as soon as possible and get out of there."

"Please don't tell John this. Just let him know that I am making progress. I might have to go to him tonight. I don't think I can get out of it. I just want to get my license and go to the library to do some research. I want to find out on my own what is real. Can you give me the okay to drive? Right now John brings me here and he wants me call him as soon as I get home. I feel like he is watching me too closely."

"I'll do better than that, I'll call John right now. He left his work number with the office and I have it in your files. John Marcus please," he said, after dialing his number. "Hi John, Dr. Newman here. You asked me to call you with an update on your wife. I just had a session with her. I wanted to let you know that we are making progress. She seems well enough to go on with her life, but she is still having some confusion. Just be patient with her, and agree with whatever she tells you. It's important that she still doesn't get stressed out. Yes, I do think she can, and I believe it will be alright if she drives as long as it's just around town some," I heard him say as he looked at me and winked.

"He wanted to know if it's okay to make love, so just make him contented until you find a way out." he said, as I got up to leave.

After leaving the Doctor I decided to walk the five blocks home rather than calling a cab. I felt better than I have in a long time. I still wanted to find a way to keep from making love to John, but if it meant getting my license, I would just have to endure it. I knew that Miim would be upset if I slept with John, but I hope he understands the reason why.

The sun was shining, and the air was fresh and crisp. A gentle breeze blowing my hair. I couldn't help thinking about Miim and Dani and our walks through the park. I had an unusual desire to walk through our park. It was several more blocks away but I wanted the exercise, so I decided to go for it. About a block or two into the park, I thought I had better take a rest. The baby was not showing yet but I tire easier. I don't get as sick as I did with Dani but I do have other health issues and knew that I could not be out long. I laid my hand across my stomach and felt a little movement. "You're going to take after your father aren't you?" I said aloud.

When I looked up, I saw a man in a distance. He was holding a little girl. *Miim, Dani,* I thought. *It's them, I know it's them.* I got up to walk fast in their direction, but they are so far away. "Miim, Miim," I shouted, but they could not hear me. "I'm over here Miim," this time screaming. I had to get to them. *Please God, let me get to them,* my heart and soul were screaming out. I got to about where they were standing, but no one was there. I looked all around but there were several directions they could have gone. I saw a family with small children, including a little girl, sitting at a picnic table. I asked them if they saw a man with a little girl standing near here. They said they have been the only ones here. I turned around to walk back, feeling sad, thinking it must have been that man with his little girl that I saw, or am I really crazy? No one seems to know anything about my being missing. If only Carrie was still here, she is the only one that I could completely trust. She is the only one that could tell me what happened before the fire. Tears streamed down my face as I walked home. I was thinking that John would be calling me soon and I had to hurry. I thought about Brian and wondered how much Carrie told him. He is back to work, but I need to find a way to talk to him without John knowing it.

When I got back, I found a message from John to call him. He scolded me, telling me he had been worried.

"I'm sorry, I was feeling a little cooped up. I felt so good that I wanted to take a walk through the park," I said trying to pacify him. He couldn't talk long so he said he would talk to me tonight.

That night John let me know that I should not go anywhere unless he knew where I was. He let me know that he is still concerned about me. He gave me my license and he told me that my Doctors gave me the okay to make love with him. I told him that I was sure that I would be fine after I rested up tonight after my long walk.

"I guess I was feeling happy about going on with my life and I decided to walk over to the park. I think I over did it. I want to go to bed now. I promise I will be rested more tomorrow." *I have to get to the library tomorrow,* I thought. *I can not avoid him any longer without him being suspicious.*

"Tonight Angie, you go rest up for now, I want you with me tonight."

"John, it's been a long time, I want everything to be perfect," I lied. "Tomorrow I will move my things back in our room. We will be back in each other's arms in no time. Do you remember we used to look up at the stars and it was so romantic? We use to have candlelight dinners before the children came. I want our first time back together to be like that, so we can get that romantic feeling back again."

"Okay, I get it, you want it to be a date huh?" He was smiling and he seemed to be going along with it.

"I would like to go to the mall tomorrow. I want to get a couple of things for our date. It will feel good getting out to do a little shopping," I told him. "Is there anything I can get for you?"

"No Honey, just don't get tired. We are moving you in our room tomorrow. I want to show you how much I have changed." He came over to me and put his arms around me and held me tightly next to him and he kissed me, at first tenderly and then with more passion. I could tell he did not want to let me go and I knew he wanted me now. *Please God, don't let him feel me shaking inside.*

"Okay John, tomorrow, as soon as I rest up tonight. I promise I won't over do it at the mall. I have some things planned for us tomorrow," I said, smiling up at him.

He did not release his hold on me, and looked down at me and kissed me again. All I could do was respond to his kiss and smile. It was the only way I could be believable, although I felt sick to my stomach. He stroked my face, and I was afraid that he was not going to stop and I became frightened. I thought about the night that he was about to rape me. I put my arms around him and gave him a little squeeze, although, I was afraid that he was not going to believe me about our little date. He looked at me as if he was checking out what I was thinking. He again stroked my face then he kissed me again lightly, released me and walked away. I'm not sure what he was thinking, but I prayed that he believed me. *Just one more day.*

The next day I went straight to the library as soon as John went to work. After getting information on what I was looking for, the librarian gave me a couple of discs to put on the computer. It took about fifteen minutes of searching, and then I found it. In bold letters, FOUR

LOCAL WOMEN MISSING! My heart was racing as I read on. Three women reported missing from the mall area on Wednesday. Tammie Benson, Angela Marcus and Gina King, all disappeared around the same time. The forth woman disappeared near Timm's Grocery. Foul play has been suspected. The article went on to say what we were wearing and other details. I found myself shaking, but I searched farther. Everyday, from that point, there was an article about our being missing, and a link between the four of us. Other articles reported husbands were accused. Others saying husbands have been cleared of murdering their wives. I read on, and found out that other states had women missing. Some said that over two hundred women could not be accounted for, and theories of what could have happened to them. It caused a lot of people to panic and women mostly stayed indoors. After a couple of months of articles, our story phased out, nothing more, we were forgotten. I kept searching subsequent issues anyway hoping something would pop up somewhere about us. I brought a snack and some water so that I wouldn't have to leave. I just wanted to gather all the information that I could. After about three hours the only articles I found was about a woman that was found dead in the woods. It was first believed it was one of us, but later proved it was someone from another state and dumped there. Another one said that it had been discovered that over three hundred women from different states went missing around the same time as we did. I was getting tired so I decided that I would come back again the next day to continue my search. I wanted to find out more about John's affair since he got rid of my pictures of him and Kay. Right now I was feeling anger.

John has been lying to me. Apparently, so was my friend Grant and I intended to find out why. I took a copy of the article with my name in it, and headed over to see Grant.

"What's wrong with you Angie, pushing your way in here like that?" Grant said this harshly after I told the desk clerk that I was going in, and no one is stopping me.

"You've been lying to me Grant, and I want to know why."

"What are you talking about?"

"Don't lie to me any more Grant, I am through with your's and John's lies. I went to the library and found articles about the disappearance of four women, and I just happen to be one of them," I said as I threw the copy of my article down on his desk. "And later, articles said that over three hundred women were missing. Does all this sound familiar? You and John both were making me feel like I was going crazy. Here's the proof Grant, now tell me the truth. Do you think you are helping me by lying to me?"

He got up to close the door. "Angie," he said, looking down like he did not want to have to tell me anything. "John thought it would be best if you didn't know everything now. You have been through a lot, and the less we told you the better off you were. Don't you see we want to protect you? Your Doctors did not want us to tell you any more than we had to. They told us it would be less shock to the brain if you remember things on your own. What did you find out Angie?"

"Why don't you just tell me the truth Grant, and then I will tell you what I found out. The truth Grant! The

Doctors told you not to tell me things but that doesn't mean you had to lie when I asked you about it. Why are you protecting John?"

"Calm down Angie. Does John know you are here?"

"No, but I will be talking to him tonight, and it better match everything you tell me. No wonder I am so mixed up. I feel like a fool. Between you and John, you try to keep me that way." I was crying now, and Grant gave me a few minutes before he began. He took a step towards me, but I threw my hands up, motioning him to stop.

"Come on, calm down. How about if I come over tonight and talk to you and John?" Grant appeared nervous. He picked up a pencil and toyed with it and threw it back down on his desk. "I don't want to make you any worse than you are."

"Is that what you are trying to do? Trying to protect me? I'm fine, I have the Doctors report, and I can go on with my life. Right now Grant, tell me now! I thought you were my friend."

"Okay, sit down," he started as I was taking a seat. "You were missing for about two and a half years. No one believes your story about where you were. John thinks you ran off with someone and got pregnant and had to stay away for awhile. He thinks you only came back to get the kids. He doesn't believe what you are telling him about aliens, and being on another planet. Can you blame him? He has been trying to find out who it is that took you. During the time you were missing, he tried in vain to find you."

"But, why couldn't he have told me that much? No wonder he doesn't believe anything I tell him. He is acting suspicious of me."

"Angie, the story you told us about another planet would start a panic. We were told to put a cap on it until further investigation. We just can't put your story in the news. Either people are not going to believe you and want to put you away, or the ones that do believe you will hide in their homes the rest of their lives. My job depends on what you say. It was easier to just hush this up. John suggested that we just let people think we really don't know what happened to you due to your fall. We just tied the two in together." Grant picked up the pencil again, but this time he made a note on a pad.

"I guess I never thought about that. I wouldn't have believed it either if I didn't live it. No wonder John is acting strange. So, he thinks I ran off with someone, had his baby and decided after over two years I had to come back to get the kids. Grant I told you the truth when I told you I was taken by force, that is what happened. Do you believe me?"

"I believe everything you told me about your being abducted, Angie. I have every reason to, but I don't believe that aliens abducted you, although; I think it could be what your abductors wanted you to believe. I didn't believe John hurt you, it just didn't add up. He is an ass, and I never really liked him, but I don't think he would kill you. John told me the Doctors thought it would be better if you remembered things on your own. I had to go along with him. Of course he is probably afraid that you will leave again and take the kids. He does believe you had a baby that is not his. I guess he thinks you might want to try to find that child."

"Grant, what about Tammie Benson, didn't her story match mine? How can you hide all this from our town when others have the same story?"

"Tammie Benson is still missing, Angie. She never offered proof of her whereabouts. She came back long enough to steal her kids out of school and took off again. The only one who saw her was the principal. Everyone just thinks she ran off with another man. I'm not doubting, they led you to believe they are from another planet. A lot of the other missing women never did come back or they were never reported. Some that did come back left their husbands again. There has never been any real proof of aliens."

"Tammie's husband was abusive, and she went back with them on her own. Grant, I didn't know her before all this happened. I had never met her before. All the women that were with me wanted to stay with the men that took them. Doesn't that tell you how wonderful these men were?"

"I know, I believe everything before your fall you think is true. You were in a coma for so long after you fell that I'm not sure even you believe everything you say."

"Grant, I told you the truth about John trying to kill me. We did have an argument, and he grabbed me up and was tearing my clothes. He was going to rape me. The phone rang, I think it was Carrie. She knew there was something wrong and that's when she came over to help me. John set the fire after I ran upstairs. He killed Carrie, maybe not meaning to, but I do believe he was trying to kill me. I think, if he get's mad enough, he will try again. You have to believe me Grant. Please don't wait until he accomplishes it before you believe me. I can't explain why neighbors saw him coming home after the fire started, unless they just didn't know he was there in the first place. He was home, and probably left again and came back for some reason or other. That's probably when he was seen. I guess he changed his mind about killing me or maybe he thought the job would have been done. I think he came back, and was surprised to find me on the back patio with a cracked skull and pretended to save my life."

"I do believe you now Angie, and I'm sorry I doubted you. We have been investigating what you told us and everything fits."

"Thanks, but I need to stay with him for now. If I leave he will suspect that you are on to him. I need to finish this on my own, but I plan to confront him tonight."

"Let me come with you, Angie."

"No, I will call you if I need you."

"Just be careful. I don't think John will do anything tonight but remember you are pregnant."

I left Grant's office feeling accomplished, and I felt so much better knowing that he believes me. At least about John trying to kill me. Secretly, I think he believed the part about aliens taking me, but I understood why he had to keep that part to himself. I'm sure, even more now after talking to Grant, that Miim is real, and so is my little girl. Now, I had to go home to face John. At least now I won't have to make love to him and I knew he would not have waited any longer. I wondered if he would tell me the truth, or will he go on lying to me? John makes up stories to satisfy his own wants and needs. I realize now he wants to keep me confused. I just pray he won't try to hurt me again, but I knew that this was my only chance to get out. He, more than likely, told my parents that I'm insane so they will be sure not to let me have the kids. Even if Miim is not here anymore, I had to leave, or make sure John does.

John came home early that evening. I wondered if Grant called him and told him what happened at his office, but I dismissed that idea. He probably came home early to start our date. I really think Grant wants to catch John, but does not have enough evidence.

John seemed very happy to see me, and he was ready for us to be together.

"I finished early today. I thought I would take my girl out to dinner," he said in a jolly mood.

"First, I want you to tell me the truth about every lie that you have been telling me. You know, the ones about my being missing. I guess Grant called you, and told you I went to the library to do some research. You might as well tell me the truth."

"Angie, Honey, you know that I couldn't talk much about it. For God's sake, you were in a coma for quite a few weeks. I had to make sure you were well. The Doctors told me that I should tell you as little as possible. Even Grant wanted me to keep it to myself." He looked shocked and I knew that he didn't want to tell me anymore.

"Okay, I'll buy that for now, although, I'm not sure what I believe is true. You guys had me so confused that I didn't know what happened. Now tell me exactly what you think happened."

"What I think is, we were having a few problems in our marriage, and someone, I guess his name is Miim, weird name, talked you into going off with him. You left me, and your kids for someone else. I don't believe you were ever abducted. You were talking like you were taken to another world or something. You came back after two years, and told me you had another kid by him. Of course I was mad as hell. What I want to know is where he is now, and do you intend to go back with him? You told me you still love this guy, so naturally I'm concerned. That's one of the reasons I didn't tell you. I want you, Angie. I can't let this guy come in and ruin our marriage. We need to fix us. All this stuff you told us about saving another planet, and producing kids is stupid. You have to quit telling that story Angie. Your Doctors will have you committed."

"*Miim, Oh thank God Miim you are real, I didn't make you up. You will come back for me someday. The baby I'm carrying, it's Miim's.*

"The truth John, is this your baby I'm carrying? You know I will have a DNA done. The truth will come out sooner or later anyway."

"No, but I will except it as my own. I promise Angie, I will love this kid the same as I love my own," John said, as he shifted from one foot to another. "Just please say you will stay and make this marriage work."

"You were about to rape me before the fire started John and the phone rang. You didn't think about this baby when you grabbed me, and you were hurting me. Come on, the truth!"

"I would never hurt you, but you are my wife, does that sound like rape? I was mad Angie, and hurt. I had no idea you were pregnant until you were in a coma." His face was getting red, his voice louder.

"You lit the fire that almost killed me."

"Come on, Honey, do you think I would actually kill you?"

"Yes, if you are hurt or angry enough, I think you would. Admit it, you lit the fire."

"Yes, but I didn't think it would catch like that. I came back, I tried to save you, remember?"

"Did you? or did you just let them believe you did? Tell me what really happened."

"When I lit the fire, I left, and came back. I was hurt and mad but I didn't want you to die. I love you."

"Who really saved me? It wasn't you was it? There was someone else there."

"No, not at first. I was doing CPR when people started showing up. I was afraid of what was going to happen. God Angie, I didn't think you would jump, I panicked."

"Who else, John? Someone else tried to save me, tell me who it was."

I don't know who it was. Some guy came out of nowhere and told me I had better continue CPR. I thought I'd seen him somewhere before. I guess a neighbor or something, anyway, he called the fire department and ambulance."

"What did he look like?"

"I don't know, it was dark, he was tall and had dark, curly hair, that's all I could make out."

Miim was there, I know it. He helped save me. Poor Miim, what he has been going through. At least now I know that he is aware that I was seriously hurt, and I could not contact him.

"How did Carrie get in there? What did she have to do with any of this?"

187

"It's not my fault she got killed Angie. I didn't do that." He thrust his hands in his pockets, jingling his change and started shifting from one foot to the other again. He appeared very nervous.

"How is it not your fault? You lit the fire."

"I swear, I didn't know she was in there and I didn't know that you would jump from the second floor window. I was going to put the fire out. I really feel bad that you got hurt. I thought I lost you."

He had tears in his eyes. He almost seemed genuine.

"That was her on the phone, wasn't it? She was calling to check up on me. She was worried and called me didn't she John? You might as well tell me the truth," I was screaming at him, crying at the same time.

"Yes, it was her, but I didn't know she would come over here."

"I understand now, she called, she saved me from being raped by you. You recognized her voice, and you told her she had the wrong number. You should have known she would recognize your voice. She knew it was you. You knew she would figure something was wrong. You should have known she would come over here to check on me. You are responsible for her death, John. You killed my best friend," I was screaming at him, sobbing uncontrollably.

"Don't be stupid, Angie. You can't pin her death on me. I didn't know she was in here, and you know that."

"Just the same you are responsible. I think we need to call Grant and tell him what is really going on here. Do you actually think the authorities are going to agree that you didn't kill Carrie?" I was much more calm as I went over to the phone.

"Come on Angie, get away from the phone. Even if you tell them, they won't do anything. You know I didn't mean for her to die. If I wanted you dead Angie, I never would have come back here to save you." His face was turning red again, and he took a step towards me. I never saw him more angry and I became afraid but I had to get this over with.

"You would have if you were afraid someone could have seen you come or leave. Grant already knows John, I was in his office today remember. I got him to tell me the truth about everything. He knows you are lying to him. He is waiting on you to make a mistake. He is expecting me to call him."

"Angie get away from the phone." He took another step toward me and I backed up with the phone still in my hand.

"What about the fire? You could be charged with arson."

"It's my house. The fire didn't destroy that much."

"No, it just killed Carrie and nearly killed me and my baby but don't worry," I said as I dialed Grant's phone number, "you'll probably get off. You are pretty influential in this town."

"Get away from the phone Angie, I mean it. You know damn well I didn't know you would jump out of the window. I didn't know that you were pregnant and I didn't know Carrie was here. Don't put your coma on me," he said, as he came closer to me. I never noticed before when he got very angry his jaws started flopping and right now, that's all I could see as he was screaming at me. I didn't hear what he was saying. I just knew he was very angry.

"What are you going to do John, rape me, kill me maybe? If you didn't do anything wrong what are you worried about?"

"Put the phone down," he looked at me with dagger in his eyes. As he spoke very hateful, I became afraid that he would hurt me. I knew he was not going to let me go. He grabbed my wrist and the phone fell to the floor. He then grabbed my hair, pulled it back until I cried out and pushed me up against the wall like he did before the fire. He got very close to my face. I could feel his anger as he slurred his words and spit came from his mouth as he started yelling at me. His mouth took on weird shapes as he started calling me names. Everything came back to me. I remember before my coma, he pulled my hair and cursed at me. I know now how stupid I have been. I gave him the benefit of my doubt, believing part of what he was telling me, although skeptical. Now I know not ever to trust him again.

"You bitch, you ran off from me. You had a bastard child, and you accuse me of doing something wrong. Yes, you bitch, I will make love to you anytime I want, and yes, I will kill you if necessary."

"John please, I'm pregnant, the baby, I will lose the baby, let me go."

"You should have thought of that before. It's not mine anyway. Damn you Angie, I tried to make it right between us. You wouldn't listen to me, now it's too late." He was screaming at me, jaws flapping even harder, as he hit me across the mouth and then he started ripping at my clothes. He was going to rape me, and I would not be able to keep him from doing it. He pulled at my jeans while I was fighting back, but I was no match for him.

He struck me again and I fell to the floor. He came down on me hard punching at me, putting his knee hard on my stomach. I was screaming in pain and again he started pulling off my jeans. There was nothing I could do but to allow him to rape me. I could no longer fight back. I had to think of my baby, and fighting back John, will only make it worse. I felt trapped and frightened.

"No other man is going to touch you again Angie, I will see to that." He spat at me again, and he put his knee on my stomach again as I screamed out in pain. His mouth came down over mine to keep me quiet.

"Let her go," A stern voice behind us said.

John looked up like a frightened animal.

Miim, it was Miim!

"You have hurt her for the last time, now get off of her."

"You again, what do you want, and what the hell are you doing in my house." John said, still very angry.

"I came for her. I said get away from her." Miim raised a weapon, and John slowly got up, and backed up with his hands raised.

"Miim, you are here," I cried.

"I'm here baby, just pick up that phone and call the police."

I got up, pulled my jeans back up, and picked up the phone, but all I wanted to do was run into his arms. He looked so big, tall, he never looked better. I love this man. I cried, I couldn't stop, I just cried while calling Grant and as I was talking to him. I couldn't stop crying.

"Now come over here to me," he said after I finished the call.

He looked at my face, and touched my mouth. He had blood on his fingers. He put his arm around my waste, and pulled me into him, while he kept the weapon in the other hand, aimed at John.

"How could you do this to her? What kind of man are you to knock around a woman like that? I ought to kill you right now."

"No Miim, please don't"

"Don't worry I won't, it's just a threat in case he ever tries to beat you or rape you again."

"She's my wife, I think you're the one that ought to get the hell out of here," John said, very disgusted with both of us.

"You better go before the police come," I said to Miim.

"I will, you take this and hold it on him. If he makes a move shoot him in the knee. Do you remember how I taught you to use this?"

"Yes"

"I will be watching and I would advise you to stay very still," he said to John. "She is very good with this weapon." Miim was bluffing but John did not know that. I have never touched a weapon in my life, nor did I know that Miim even owned one. It didn't even look like any gun that I knew of.

"Are you okay?"

"I'm Okay Miim."

"I'll be back for you."

"Is that the man that helped you save me?" I asked John as Miim went out the back door.

"That's him, and he was the one on the outside of that restaurant when we had an argument. I also caught him in your room at the hospital looking at you and talking to you. I don't trust him. I figured he was the one you ran off with."

"That's Miim, he is the one that took me in the first place. I told you the truth about that John. To bad you didn't believe me. He is from another planet. I only came back here to see if our marriage was worth saving, and get the kids if it wasn't. I know now that it isn't worth saving. I could never forgive you for cheating on me. I could never forgive you for trying to get rid of the baby just now. I will always blame you for being responsible for Carrie's death."

"You're not going to shoot me Angie." He started to make a move toward me.

"I would be very still if I were you. I'm as mad as hell right now. I'm getting tired of you smacking me around. Don't give me another excuse to make sure you never walk again."

Grant and another policeman arrived and arrested John. They saw what he had done to me.

"I'm sorry Angie," Grant approached me, and put his hand on my arm. He took the weapon away from me, and looked at it, then back at me. He knew! "Are you okay?"

"I am, I was just worried about the baby. John was about to rape me again when Miim came in and stopped him. I think John wanted to hurt me enough to get rid of the baby."

"Come on, I will take you to the hospital. I'm sorry that I didn't believe you sooner. I just didn't think John was capable of this much abuse. This guy, Miim, are you afraid of him?"

"No Grant, I love him. I'm going to get my kids and go back with him. He is a wonderful guy."

"John had me follow him one night after he left the hospital. He wanted to know where he lived. He wanted me to have him arrested, but I couldn't find a reason to take him in. He figured he was the one you ran off with. I will go and tell him that I am taking you to the hospital so he won't worry about you. Is this his gun?"

"Yes! Grant, will John be going to jail? I don't trust him."

"I don't think you will have to worry about him for a long time. I am going to have to ask you to stay around for awhile. We will need your help putting him away." Grant looked down.

I know it hurt Grant to arrest someone that has been his friend for so long. I felt bad for him. For now, I wasn't feeling anything for John. I was only feeling some pain in my stomach and prayed the baby would be okay.

"Come on, let's get you to the hospital," he said, as they took John away.

I saw John glance toward me, as they led him away. That, I dare you to cross me, glance. It gave me a frightened, sickening feeling. I was losing my balance as Grant held on to me, while leading me to his car.

I told him everything that I thought John did and this time he believed me.

CHAPTER TWELVE

Miim was there as I left the hospital the next day. He was waiting for me near a cab. I smiled and he smiled back. "Everything is okay," I said as I approached him. He walked toward me and put his arms around me. He held me so tenderly.

"Are you okay? I am so sorry, Angie."

"What for, you didn't do anything."

"That bastard almost raped you. I would have killed him if he did."

"I'm okay, really!"

"I couldn't get to you when you jumped out that window. I almost lost you. I love you so much and I almost lost you," he repeated.

"Miim, none of this is your fault, you didn't do anything. Oh Miim, after I was in a coma, everyone had me so confused. I didn't know if you were real or not. John had me believing that I was making you up in my head, and for awhile I believed him. I just kept having bad dreams and my head was hurting and I felt all mixed up.

When I realized you were real I thought you were gone. I thought you had to go back to Cribaar. I didn't know when I was going to see you or Dani again," I cried.

"It's okay honey. Everything is going to be okay now. I'm not going to let you out of my sight again as long as we are here. John will never touch you as long as I'm around. Come on, let's go back to your house so we can talk. We can decide what we'll do next," he said as he guided me to the taxi. "Grant came to me last night. I wasn't sure about him at first but I like him. He brought my weapon back, and told me he understood, but to keep it hidden. I think he knows that I am from another planet. He ask me about the weapon, and I told him."

"I'm glad you got to talk to him. I think he understands now why I have to get away from John."

"I was here at the hospital for several hours last night but they wouldn't let me see you. I didn't want to be arrested so I didn't stay. I knew you would need me. Grant was here. He stayed at the hospital for several hours to make sure you were okay."

On the drive back home Miim held me next to him, kissing my forehead. I told him a few important details of what happened since the first day I got back, including John telling everyone the baby was his.

"Baby, what baby?"

"Oh, I guess you don't know. We're going to have another baby."

"Oh gosh Sweetheart, you went through all this abuse, and you were pregnant too?"

"You don't sound too happy about it."

"But Honey, we almost lost you and Dani. We weren't going to have any more children. We weren't even suppose to come back to Earth if you were expecting a child. How did this happen?"

"Well since you are it's daddy I'm guessing you already know that answer." I could see that the cab driver had a smile on his face, as he listened in on our conversation.

"Honey, I am okay. I got checked out while I was in the hospital. The baby is fine and so am I."

"What are we having?" he asked smiling, and pulling me closer to him.

"I don't know, but we will find out together."

"I'm going to make sure that you don't do anything. I will take care of everything. You just need to take care of yourself, and I'm sorry you had to go through what you did."

"All of this time you were watching over me."

"As much as I could."

As soon as we got to my house, Miim put his arms around me again and kissed me very tenderly.

"You're all bruised and swollen," he said, as he touched my face tenderly. He then put his finger to my swollen lip and again kissed it so gently.

"I'm okay, I just want you to kiss me again." He did just that, so tenderly, as our tears mingled together.

After holding each other for awhile, I asked him where the spacecraft was and where Dani was.

"The spacecraft went back to Cribaar, but Dani and I stayed behind. I had to stay Angie," he said so sweetly. "I could never leave you. I know that my father is disappointed in me, but I love you, and I had to wait until you were well. If you decided you didn't want to come back with me, I would have told you that John tried to kill you. No way was I going to let him hurt you again. If I had to, I would have kidnapped you again. If I had known we were going to have a baby I would have gone in after you before the day of the fire. I would have tried to convince you to come with me. Now, I wish I would have."

"I didn't know that I was pregnant until I came out of the coma. John knew before I did."

"Yea, and I guess he had it all planned out that he was going to get you back by claiming the baby, and convincing you that the coma was making you crazy. He was messing with your mind Angie. How did you figure out he was lying to you?"

"I wasn't sure until I went to the library to look for articles of my disappearance. I kept feeling you. I was almost convinced he was lying to me. I went straight to Grant's office and confronted him, and he told me the truth. He had no choice. I then came home and waited for John and confronted him. That's when he turned on me. He killed Carrie, Miim. She died in that fire trying to save me. John caused her to die, and I will never forgive him."

Miim held me and let me cry. When I was feeling better I asked him about Dani.

"Terrin is here with me. He has Dani now. Terrin is trying to convince a woman to go back with him. She was already in the process of divorcing her husband. It took him much longer because the woman became ill and had to stay with her abusive husband. He didn't even try to take care of her, or her daughter. I met her Angie and she is a sweet girl. You will like her."

"But where have you been staying?"

"For a little over a month we have been staying at a hotel downtown, at your expense of course. I was getting worried that John was going to find out about it."

"He did get a bill on food and diapers, but I told him that someone needy probably used the credit card but I figured it might be you. It gave me hope for awhile, Miim. Before I came out of the coma, I thought I felt you. It seemed so real."

"It was real. I was there several times in the middle of the night, talking to you. I kept reminding you of who I was and I told you about how much our daughter missed you. I was worried that you weren't going to come out of it. I got caught the last time by your husband. Angie, I couldn't stand it you lying there and I was thinking I may never get you back," he said, as he stroked my hair, and then kissed my forehead.

"What do you mean he caught you?"

"He got there early one morning as I was talking to you. I did have his schedule figured out but that morning he was much earlier."

"I knew I felt you there, I knew it. Miim you did bring me back. I kept feeling your touch. What happened when John found you there?"

"Well, he wanted to know who I was, and what I was doing there, so I told him. Of course he wasn't pleased, and he called an emergency number on his phone. I told him I didn't do anything wrong, and I was just checking on you. He told me to leave and never come back again. He accused me of kidnapping, and he said he would have me put in jail if I came back again. I reminded him that I was the one that helped save you."

"But who did you tell him you were?"

"I told him that I was the one you were with the last couple of years, and the father of your last child. I also told him I plan to take you again. Of course I said that as I walked away."

"Miim, you could have gotten caught. If they put you in jail, I would never have known you were here. Did you come back to the hospital?"

"Yes, every night. I needed to honey. I was so worried about you, and I thought, if I kept talking to you, and tell you how much I love you, maybe you would come out of the coma. I told you I was waiting for you, and taking you back with me. I didn't get caught by John again but there was a couple of incidents that I was concerned about."

"Oh Miim, what happened?"

"Well, one night a nurse came in. I just smiled at her, and told her I just got in town. I told her I was your ex., and the father of one of your children. She just said okay. I was hoping that she bought it, and didn't report me. Of course in a way it was the truth. I didn't stay long that night. Another time, when I left you, a cop was following me as I was walking back to the hotel. I believe it was the night after John caught me in your room. I think now that it might have been Grant. It was in the middle of the night. He stayed right with me, driving very slowly behind me. I thought he was going to stop me, and ask what I was up to, but when I went on in to the hotel, he drove on."

"God Miim, what if he would have stopped you?"

"I guess I would have told him the same thing as I told the nurse, only he wouldn't have thought I was so cute, and I probably would not have gotten away with it."

"Miim, this is serious. One day I walked to the park, and I thought I saw you and Dani. I called out to you. Were you there?"

"Yes, you mean you were there? I thought I heard you, but I kept looking around and I didn't see you. I wanted to run to find you, but I had Dani with me, and that slowed me down. I'm so sorry. We were so close to each other, but we didn't know."

"I knew it, I knew it was you. I want to see Dani," I said, as I sat down on the sofa.

"Tomorrow Sweetie, we will go and spend time with her tomorrow. Right now, we need to spend time together. We have a lot to talk about, and we need to get some of your things together. We don't know when John will be back. He might pay his way out so we have to get out of here by tomorrow. We know that he won't be back tonight. This might be the last time that we are alone for awhile. Soon, you better go get cash and give up the credit card. We don't want him to find us."

"When do you think we should get the kids from my parents?"

"As soon as we know that John is convicted and sent to jail, then it will be safe to get them. We don't want to put them through any of this. We will need some place to live other than this, at least until he goes to jail. I don't trust the guy. I'm sorry we will have to stay near here. You will have to be the one that puts him away."

"When will we be going back to Cribaar?"

"Does that mean you will be going back with me?"

I teasingly threw a pillow at him. "Of course silly. You knew it all the time."

"I didn't think you could refuse my great smile and cute dimples," he said as I threw another pillow at him. It is so wonderful being with him. It didn't matter what happened as long as we were safe and we can be together.

"Miim, John was about to rape me. If it wasn't for you, it could have been a lot worse. How did you know?"

"I couldn't always be there sweetheart. I feel horrible that I got here too late the night of the fire. I was watching out for you the best I could, under the circumstances. I still had to see to our little girl. Last night I was checking up on you, and I heard him yelling at you. I heard you trying to scream, so I went in. I checked up on you every day since we have been back. If everything seemed okay, then I just left. I was upset when you left the hospital because I knew you had to go back to him. I had planned to take you out of the hospital when I found out that you were out of the coma. A few times, when I was there during the night, I couldn't get you awake. I thought at first that you were in a coma again. I asked the nurse about it and she told me they couldn't keep you calm, so they had you drugged. After that, they kept everyone out. I couldn't get back in to kidnap you." Miim stood up and was pacing nervously. "I think John was afraid that I would take you again and he arranged to have no visitors in your room."

"Oh Miim, you are so wonderful to me and I am so sorry. I should have listened to you, and trusted you right from the beginning."

"Don't worry, everything is going to be alright now. The spaceship will be back sometime next year but that should give us time to have the baby, and take care of everything," Miim said, as he sat down next to me. "Will you get a divorce from John? I want us to be married as soon as we get back. I want us to be forever." He pulled me close to him again.

I have never felt so much love for him and I wanted him right then and there. He protested, and wanted to wait until I was completely well, but I insisted that if he wanted me forever, than forever starts now. We made love, wonderful tender but passionate love.

Later, I told him that I wanted to divorce John. I also told him how John almost raped me right before the fire and how Carrie kept from it happening.

"The bastard, he didn't hurt you did he?"

"He smacked me around a little, but no, I managed to get away from him."

"It is a wonder that this baby is okay. Did you ever have to sleep with him or, anything else?"

"When I got out of the hospital I was not well enough. We both thought it would be good for me to stay in the guest room. I did sleep in our bed when I first got home, but he never touched me in that way. I think he knew we needed time, and at that time he did not push me. When we visited the kids at my parents, we were forced to sleep together because of space, but I think that was my mother's plan. Of course John tried, but I just kept making excuses. He also tried another day. It was the day he found out that someone was using our credit card. I went on up to take a shower and he was going out to the store. Before I knew it he was in the bathroom. He said he forgot to kiss me good by, but I knew what he came back for. I told him that it was to soon, and convinced him to wait until I got an okay from the Doctor and he bought it."

"I can't stand the thought of him touching you."

"Jealous!"

"Yea!"

The four of us stayed at the hotel until John was sent to jail, and then we moved back to the house. Terrin kept Dani a lot while I showed Miim around. We took our little girl to the park almost every day. I was so happy just being with them. Miim and I both, went to my parents, to pick up the kids. I figured if they met him they would see how sweet he is, and maybe they would like him, and accept him. I wanted him with me in case they gave me any problem. They did just that. They accused me sending John to jail, so that I could run away with Miim. At first, they tried to keep the children away from me. I told them unless they wanted to join John they could not keep my children from me. They even hired a lawyer and accused me of being an unfit mother. They told me that John would not have done the things he did, if I would have been a good wife. They also told me they would never forgive me for what I did to John, and they would not accept Miim, Dani, or the baby. I figured I could be out of here before they could get this case to court. Miim tried to tell them that John almost killed me, and was the cause of Carrie's death, but they already made up their minds not to listen to anything he had to say. Needless to say, we gathered up the kids with their belongings and left the same day.

John was convicted of attempted rape, abuse, manslaughter, and third degree arson. He would be in prison for the next ten years. The hardest part was telling the children, but after explaining to them what he did to me, they understood. They were happy with being back with me. They were excited about going to live on another planet. They were just young enough to be intrigued about the whole thing. They understood why their father went to prison. Andrew even testified that John got him to lie. I know they love their father, and someday we will bring them back to see him, but they also got a chance to know Miim and they think he is great. Miim treats all the kids as his own, and showers all of us with love, and gives us lots of attention. The children call him Daddy Two, and he loves it.

The easiest part was getting Ann's children. Her parents believed us when Miim showed them her pictures and the letter she gave to him. They saw how happy she was, and they were happy she was safe. We didn't tell them she was on a different planet, but we did tell them she was about to have another child and wanted to stay in hiding for fear of what her husband would do. Her parent's health was not good, so they were unable to keep the kids much longer. They were relieved to get them away from their father. He was running around, partying and ignoring the children, acting as if they didn't even exist. They were afraid of him and he would beat them for almost nothing, especially when he was drunk. We got a video of her parents for her, and we told them that she should be able to get back in a few months and find a way to visit them. We decided it would be easier on the children if we went ahead and got them, and to get them use to us. They were sweet and they were excited about going to see their mother.

We went to visit Adam, and his new wife Julie. I missed their wedding, but the children told me all about it. I instantly loved Julie, she is so perfect for Adam. Miim at first did not want to go. I guess he felt a little awkward after the ordeal with my parents, but when he got to know Adam he liked him. When we first got there we did not tell them that Miim was from another planet. They knew he was different, but they did not want to mention his accent, worried they would make him feel uncomfortable. When they found out they had so many questions and were so intrigued. Adam told me later that he liked him and said that he was right for me.

I went to see Brian before the trial began and to fill him in on what happened with Carrie. I blamed myself, and he blamed himself for letting her go out. He said he wished he would have gone with her.

"It's not your fault Brian," I told him sternly. "We have to stop blaming ourselves. John did this, and he will pay. I will never forgive him." He thanked me for coming, and I held him as he sobbed. Brian also testified at the trial and, I believe his testimony is what help put John away.

We decided all of us, including Terrin, and Ann's children, would stay at the house until we could sell it, or until it was time for us to leave for Cribaar. We lived off selling valuable paintings and sculptures that John got for me over the years. We would have Brian and Grant over, now and then, and both of them got to know Miim and understood how I fell hard for him. They all became good friends, and both Brian and Grant confessed they never did like John. Alyssa is excited to have a little sister to play with, and a new baby on the way. Andrew taught

Terrin how to play video games, and both had a good time. Terrin's new girlfriend, Darlene and her daughter Beth Ann, moved in with us. We quickly became good friends, and Beth Ann, who was four years old, fit right in with our family. Darlene was also badly abused along with Beth Ann. Terrin did not take her from her home, he got to know her by accident. He was joking around with her at a grill where she worked, and eventually found out, by the bruises on her, that she was abused. He talked her into leaving her husband for him. At first she didn't know that Terrin was from another planet and was reluctant to go, but after I told her about it she is excited about going. We are keeping her hidden in the house until we leave for fear her husband will come after her. She and Terrin are in love and are very sweet together.

In a few months, we will be going back to Cribaar, that far away small, hidden, but perfect planet. I think back on the last few years of my life, and the amazing story that I want to tell, although; not many people will believe. I am very excited about going back and being with Miim and loving him, and all of our children. I am so happy and I couldn't wait to return to our destiny.

John is not happy about my leaving with the children, but I told him after he gets out in ten years, they could decide where they want to live.

Within a few weeks, I will have another little baby girl, and I think Miim is more excited about it than I am. He wanted me to name her like I did Dani. I assured him that I would come up with something. I had a much easier pregnancy than I did with Dani. We figured it might have had something to do with being on another planet.

One day as were walking through the park with all seven children and one on the way. I was thinking how many people thought all of them were ours. They would just look at us and smile.

"The baby will be here soon, Sweetheart," Miim said. "Don't you think you should pick out a name?"

"I have!"

"What is it?" he asked excitedly, as he grabbed my hand. "Please don't make it too terrible," he teased.

"Kari, after your mom Karis and my friend Carrie"

"Perfect, that's perfect," he said smiling down at me. "Angie do you see why I love you so much? You amaze me. Kari, I love that name. I love you, I just love my whole family."

"Do you see why I love you so much?" I said smiling up at him. "And you thought it was your great smile, and cute dimples."